THE SPIDER:
SATAN'S SIGHTLESS LEGION

THE **MASTER OF MEN!**

SPIDER®

SATAN'S
SIGHTLESS LEGION

By Grant Stockbridge

STEEGER BOOKS • 2020

CHAPTER 1
A PERILOUS TRAIL

WENTWORTH TWISTED the Hispano roadster around three corners in rapid succession, taking the turns with whistling tires. Afterward, he drove straight and fast with his lights out. But presently, in the rear vision mirror, he glimpsed a pair of headlamps pacing him again, with the steady tenacity of a trailing wolf.

Wentworth nodded to the boy beside him. "You were right, Jim," he said quietly. "They're following us."

The boy fought against the fright that made his face pale, that widened his eyes. "Can't you shake them, sir? Gosh, this car oughta do a hundred!"

"A hundred and twenty-five," Wentworth amended. "But I don't want to shake them."

He switched on his lights again and drove steadily, his gray-blue eyes narrowed a little, his lips smiling. There was nothing bitter or angry about his smile. So always did he welcome battle, with leaping blood, with an eagerness like hunger. And he knew that battle impended....

"Tell me again," Wentworth asked the boy, "just what happened. Begin with this morning."

As he listened to the answer, his eyes glanced alternately to the road again and to the trailing car. Whoever followed, appar-

ently had no intention of overtaking him just yet… A frown of concentration made a vertical crease between his eyes.

"… Sis washed out her eyes like she does every morning with a little glass cup," Jimmie said. "At first there wasn't anything

wrong, but in a few minutes, she started screaming. She couldn't see, Mr. Wentworth! She couldn't see a damn thing!"

It was clear enough, Wentworth thought, that some one had

wanted Linda Carroll away from the Schultz Grocery Company's central offices today, or had wanted her usual substitute to take her place. Linda's eyes had improved after a short while, but still her sight was far from perfect, so she had sent Sue Moran, her fiancé's sister, as her substitute to Schultz's. And this afternoon, Schultz's had been robbed of the week-end collections, nearly twenty thousand dollars. The bandits, in addition to their guns, carried huge atomizers which they sprayed in the faces of their victims. Five persons had been blinded and in their writhing agony were utterly helpless. When the bandits rushed away, Sue Moran also vanished. No one knew whether or not she was in league with them, or was being held as hostage.

Jimmy, however, had his own idea. "She's in cahoots with them," Jim said violently. "Both her and that big palooka Sis wants to marry. I wish I was big enough to...."

Wentworth flashed the boy a brief smile. A spunky kid, all right, he had taken the poisoned eyewash which had blinded his sister's eyes to the police. "I'm president of the Washington Street Spider Club," he had told the police, "and I know the crooks blinded my sister so Sue Moran could help them. It was a well-organized plot."

And Police Commissioner Kirkpatrick had refused to see him!

Wentworth's eyes narrowed a little at the thought. Strange behavior for Stanley Kirkpatrick whose sympathies always went out to boys, who was meticulous about paying personal attention to such complaints. But that strange refusal was of a piece with a number of Kirkpatrick's other recent actions, all peculiar, out of character, and….

"There!" cried Jim. "There's our apartment. Gosh, I hope Sis is all right! I didn't want to leave her, but I was just doing my duty as one of the Spider club."

Wentworth said softly, "Yes, I understand." He circled the block to park, then, walking back, he paused, in the full light from the buildings entrance.

"They sure saw you, Mr. Wentworth!" Jim cried excitedly. "Those men following in that car saw you!"

Wentworth stopped in the shadow of one of the pilasters that lined the walls of the foyer. "I *wanted* them to see me, Jim! Now, you go up the stairs, out of sight. Don't show yourself until you hear me call you."

Jim grabbed Wentworth's arm with both hands. "Gosh no, don't you do that!" he cried. "Those guys will have guns and maybe some of that stuff they blind people with. Hey, look, let me stay…."

Wentworth clapped him on the back. "Up the stairs, Jimmy! Quickly, or you'll spoil my plan!"

JIM TURNED and scuttled up the steps. He was heavy for a boy of fifteen, scarcely tall enough to carry his hundred and forty pounds. Wentworth caught a glimpse of his white face as he made the stairway turn. His freckles stood out as brilliant as blood spots…. In the dim foyer Wentworth's hands strayed to the butts of two forty-five caliber automatics that rested in clip holsters beneath his arms. He drew one and mechanically checked it over, full clip, cartridge in the chamber…. He

5

thumbed the safety into place, shoved the gun into its holster.

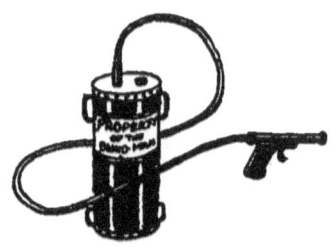

The shout that came from the steps was shrill with fright. It was Jim, and his voice broke crazily. "They got me, Mr. Wentworth. Watch Sis—" His voice choked off, and there was a harsh scuffle of feet.

It took Wentworth four leaping strides to reach the foot of the steps that curved upward, another five to reach the first platform. He went around the corner gun-first, the safety off his automatic. The stairs were empty.

Careless of danger, Wentworth bounded on, reached the head of the flight and dived across the hall. He rolled as he landed on his shoulders, came up with his gun ready. This hall was empty, too!

Blank doors, each with its metal number, faced him on all sides, as empty of meaning as idiots' faces. With an oath, Wentworth sprang to the nearest and bent to listen. Damn it, a strong boy like Jim could not be kidnaped and carried out of sight so quickly! It wasn't possible!

Wentworth sprang to the next door, the next… Then he stiffened, hearing a scream that came from above—a woman's cry. Though it was warped by pain, Wentworth made out the words: "Help! *Jimmy!* Oh, help me—"

There was no doubt in Wentworth's mind as he raced upward that the cry came from Jim Carroll's sister, Linda. The men who had seized Jim must have carried him on up the stairs and were now attacking the girl, too. Unknowingly, the brother and sister must possess some clue to the men who were using this blinding spray.

As Wentworth reached the fifth floor the screaming died out.

He started up the stairs, changed his mind abruptly, and raced along the hall toward the dull red light which marked the fire escape exit. It was the work of seconds to throw up the window and climb the iron-slatted steps to the sixth-floor level. The shades had been drawn, but there was a slit beneath one.

Through that, he saw why Jim's sister had ceased to scream.

There was a gag wedged between her teeth and the two men who crouched over her had bound her arms behind her back. As Wentworth peered in, the men thrust Linda Carroll toward the outer door.

With swift fingers Wentworth snatched from an inner pocket the black mask he always carried with him. He placed it over his eyes, rose to his feet. His elbow smashed the window glass, sent the shade flapping upward with a noise of miniature machine guns. He stepped lightly through the opening, an automatic in each hand.

The two men were dragging Linda Carroll forward. Wentworth had noticed and calculated upon that fact. He laughed *softly*, and the sound came from his lips flatly, mocking and challenging the thugs.

One of them sprang behind the girl and whipped out a revolver. It was a trick that would have meant death to any less steady man than Wentworth. His left automatic merely crashed twice. The first shot caught the man's right fist as he shoved out his gun to shoot, the forty-five caliber bullet hit with a force equal to a quarter-ton in foot-pounds. The gunman screamed, was whirled off balance by the impact. Wentworth's second bullet stopped the scream. It smashed his skull.

The other hood threw up his hands. His gun thudded to the floor and he chattered out a plea for mercy. The girl was prone on the floor. For a moment, Wentworth thought she might have been brushed by his bullet, but as he watched she rolled over on her back. Suddenly, Wentworth swore—a harsh oath of horror. For the girl's eyes were wide open and staring at him, yet she saw nothing. There was no iris, no pupil in her eyes. The entire eyeball was a glistening, opaque and sightless white!

Wentworth strode past her and seized the man he had left alive. The thugs face glistened with sweat. There were ugly, panicked twitchings about his mouth.

"God!" he chattered. "God! Honest, I didn't have a thing to do with it, mister. It was him!" He jerked his head toward the dead gangster. "It was him, I tell you, who planted the stuff in her eyewash!"

WENTWORTH'S EYES, behind the slits of his mask, were blazing. Slowly, he holstered one gun and slid his fingers into his vest pocket. They drew out a slim, platinum cigarette lighter. With his other gun holding the man, he stooped beside the slain killer. He touched the base of the lighter to the dead man's cheek. For an instant, the dead flesh showed nothing. Then, with the abruptness of magic, a design in rich vermilion sprang out on the flash. The hood shrieked, cringed against the wall.

"God, oh God!" he whimpered. "Don't kill me, too, Spider. For God's sake, Spider. *For—God's sake!*"

That tiny vermilion spot bore the hairy likeness of a spider that was poised to attack, its poison fangs ready to strike! And the gunman,

with all the rest of the Underworld, knew the awful import of that seal. It meant that this grim, mocking man in the mask, was none other than the swift lone wolf of justice whom all the criminal world hated and feared—the Spider!

The seal was no masquerade. Wentworth was secretly the avenger from whom criminals at once shrank and sought to kill. He did not often expose himself thus in his own identity, but there was need for haste. This man must be intimidated into immediate speech, and there was no time to be lost. The men who had followed him and Jim through the city streets were undoubtedly closing in, or else waiting below with ready guns. And the police would not be long in coming. Windows were banging up everywhere, men shouting. The shots had given the alarm.

Linda, hands still bound behind her, struggled to her feet and Wentworth sprang to help her. His gun covered the cowering gangster as with the other hand he removed her gag.

"They've got Jim!" Linda cried. "They told me they had Jim, and I had to go...."

"I know," Wentworth said quietly. His tone did not change as he addressed the gunman, but there was the hardness of granite in his eyes. "Where were you to take your prisoner?" he demanded.

The gunman dropped on his knees. He had the thin, pointed face of a wolf and his small eyes darted about the room. "Please," he pleaded, "if I tell you, the Blind Man will murder me. As God is alive, it's the truth. He'll kill me—he'll kill you...."

From the window behind Wentworth, a man spoke drawlingly. "It's the law, Spider! Just drop that gun! Hoist your hands easy, and you won't get hurt none... Right now!"

CHAPTER 2
THE BLIND MAN

NOT THE menace of the gun he knew must be leveled at his back, but three magic words held Richard Wentworth, alias the Spider, a helpless prisoner. "It's the Law!" the man had said, and the Spider did not fight the law, did not fire upon its minions. In his efforts to bring justice to many of those the police could not touch, he often went outside the law. He had killed—but it was the execution of many men who richly deserved it. He had committed robberies when his failure to do so might have brought innocent people to harm. But against the police, he was disarmed.

Nothing could change that—not even his recognition of the fact that his capture now, in his own identity behind the thin protection of the mask, meant his own death and disgrace. The Richard Wentworth whom the world knew was a wealthy clubman, a philanthropist and dilettante of the arts. He had friends in the highest circles… Which would avail him nothing if he were identified behind this mask with a dead man at his feet, with the Spider's seal upon the slain man's forehead!

"Drop that gun!" the man at the window ordered again. "I'll count three and then I'll shoot. There's just as much reward for you dead as alive!"

"Oh, that's cruel!" gasped the girl. "They were kidnaping me and the Spider saved me!"

"*One…*" said the policeman.

"Shoot him!" cried the gunman. "He killed my buddy there! What the dame says is hooey!"

"*Two….*"

"Oh, you mustn't," whimpered the girl. "I won't let you! I won't…."

Wentworth heard her stumbling, blind footsteps as she tried to rush between him and the bullet, but she was moving in the wrong direction. Men were pounding at the locked outer door of the apartment now. The girl was crying piteously. Wentworth heard the policeman at the window suck in a deep breath.

"Last chance, Spider!"

"Go to hell, copper!"

"*Three….*"

Then Wentworth, with a sudden, convulsive lunge, pitched forward. Before the policeman could squeeze the trigger he hit the floor on top of the body of the man he had killed, whipped over it and fired, all in one continuous blur of action. The unerring accuracy of his guns, which he had practiced years to acquire,

11

stood him in excellent stead. His bullet smashed the gun from the plain clothes man's hand without even searing the flesh!

The Spider did not wait to see the effect of the shot. He continued his wild roll on the floor, ready for the gunman's attack. He stared upward... It wasn't necessary to shoot. The policeman's bullet had smashed into the gunman's body just below the breast bone and hurled him back against the wall, pinning him there, writhing.

As Wentworth stared, the gunman bounced. His knees, waist and neck relaxed, his arms dangled and he hit the floor in a limp huddle, dead.

Deliberately, Wentworth got to his feet as the policeman scrambled through the window.

"Smash in the door!" he shouted. "The Spider's in here! Cover the fire escape!"

While the man rushed forward, Wentworth stooped over the second hood and pressed a seal to his forehead. He had ample time to sidestep the policeman's awkward swipe with a black-jack. The man shouted again, but the crashing blows on the door drowned out his words. Wentworth ducked under another swing, crossed a knockout right neatly to the jaw. He paused a moment beside the girl.

"The police will take care of you," he whispered. "Insist on their putting you in jail. It's the only safe place. I'm going to find Jim!"

"I will, and God bless you, Spider!" the girl whispered. "Oh, God bless you!"

WENTWORTH CLIMBED out of the window and a

policeman in the yard below opened up with a revolver. Spurts of red fire stabbed toward him. There was open-work in the steel fire escape platform between him and that gun, but nothing short of a miracle would permit a bullet to miss all the steel and hit him... On the fifth floor he ducked into the hallway and ran, light-footed, to a door that opened on an incinerator chute. Down it he threw coat, hat, mask, collar and tie. He rumpled his hair and ran noisily down the steps.

"The Spider!" he cried shrilly, his voice sharp with fright. "The Spider's in my apartment!"

On the third floor, a young policeman in uniform bounded into his path and seized him by the arms. "Where?" he demanded. "Where's this Spider? Show me!"

Wentworth wrenched free of him. "Show you, hell!" he squeaked. "I ain't paid to fight the Spider! You're paid to protect me. Go up and get him!"

The cop looked at him contemptuously. "Okay, okay, cream-puff... What apartment?"

"Five-C," Wentworth told him.

The cop yelled below stairs. "The Spider's in 5-C. Watch the dumb-waiter. I'm going up!"

Three other policemen went bounding past Wentworth toward the upper floors, giving him no more than a glance.

His eyes wild, his hair disordered, Wentworth made himself pant hoarsely as he ran down to the first floor....

"The Spider come busting in through the window!" he told the sergeant on the first floor, "and he says to me, 'Keep your mouth shut!' I says to him, 'Like hell I will! Who the hell do you think you are!' He says, 'I'm the Spider, that's who I am,' and I says, 'Who do you think is afraid of you, Spider?' and he says to me, he says...."

"Oh, stow it!" the sergeant ordered brusquely. "Get the hell out of here before the Spider does come and get you!"

Wentworth scuttled out, peering back over his shoulder. The sergeant grinned briefly after him and then turned to shout orders to his men.

On the street, Wentworth turned to see a young man struggling with two hefty policemen.

"Now, take it easy, buddy," Wentworth heard one of the cops grumble. "I'm telling you everything's all right!"

"But I heard shots, I tell you!" the man cried. "And there's a window broken in Linda's apartment. Damn it, man! We're going to be married, don't you understand!"

"Linda? Linda Carroll," the cop's voice rose in question.

"Sure, Linda Carroll!" The young man wasn't looking at them, but at the door they wouldn't let him enter. "For God's sake, man, weren't you ever...."

"Then you must be Hal Moran," the cop said laboriously.

"That's right! That's right!" the young man caught the cop's arms. "You see now why I got to go in there!"

RICHARD WENTWORTH

Wentworth saw the glance that passed between the officers. One of them drew out a pair of handcuffs and snapped them on Hal Moran's wrists.

"Hey!" Moran yelled. "What the hell....!"

The cop nodded at him. "The inspector wants to see you, fellah," he said. "Your sister and your girl friend helped the crooks rob Schultz's, and...."

Hal Moran thrust a face that was suddenly white into the broader, ruddier face of the cop. "You lie!" he shouted. "You lie like hell!"

The cop chuckled a little. "Slow down, hard guy," he said. "It ain't me that says it. It's the inspector. Try calling him a liar. Just try it!"

Wentworth's lips twisted a little; Jim had been pretty sure Moran and his sister were guilty, but it was foolish to talk of Linda, who had been blinded by that awful spray. His eyes narrowed. Guilty, or not, it would be a good play to get Moran loose from the cops. If he were guilty, it would give Wentworth an in with the bandits. If he were innocent, then Wentworth was in a spot. It would be hard to prove that he wasn't involved.

Wentworth stepped close and jabbed the muzzle of an automatic, snatched from under his vest, into the belly of the policeman. He jammed it hard and he chose the spot where a punch would lay a man cold on the pavement, the solar plexus. The policeman doubled over and his companion yelped, "Here, what the hell...."

Wentworth lifted a left fist twelve inches to the man's jaw, grabbed Moran's arm. "Come on, run like hell!" he snapped.

THE HISPANO was around the block. Wentworth got behind the wheel and whirled in a tight U-turn. The sounds of pursuit died rapidly away behind. Hal Moran sat stiffly beside

Wentworth, glancing at him suspiciously from time to time.

"Linda's all right," Wentworth told him. "I was on my way up to see her when the Spider killed two guys who were trying to snatch her. Jim asked me to go."

Moran settled back against the cushions, sighed. "Gee, I'm glad to hear Linda's all right, anyway. That dumb cop, saying Linda... Say, how are her eyes!"

Wentworth felt pain like a weight about his heart. That lovely girl with her sightless, white eyes! "I don't know," he said quietly. "Jimmy said they were better."

Moran held out his wrists, "Can you get these off!"

Wentworth nodded. "Easily, but we'll have to get under a good light."

The boy fumbled out cigarettes two-handed and lighted one awkwardly. He had clean, strong features and tanned skin. His brown, bare head was a sprawling tangle of wavy hair. A nice looking chap, clean-cut, but worried now. Wentworth studied him with quick glances. He had been wrong to think of this fine boy as guilty....

"I've been damned near nuts," Moran confided when the cigarette got going. "Those bandits kidnaped Sue, and when I got to Linda, there's cops and shooting and her window is smashed in. I even saw a kid I thought was Jimmy carried into an ambulance...."

17

Wentworth put on brakes so sharply that Moran lurched forward and cracked his head on the windshield.

"What's the big idea?" he demanded, his voice frightened.

"Tell me about it," Wentworth bit out. "What about the kid and the ambulance?"

Moran stared, his mouth tight. "God, you mean it *was* Jimmy? It was when the cops first got there and were sneaking around, sort of quiet. These two men came down the steps with somebody on a stretcher. I thought it was a kid. The cops asked some questions, then let them go through and the ambulance drives off. And then I hear shooting upstairs…."

Wentworth leaned toward him. "The police were there before the shooting?" he asked quietly.

Moran nodded.

Wentworth said: "Thank you." His words were soft; his brain was racing. If the police had been there *before* the shots, it meant that the men who had followed him to the scene whom he had thought crooks, were probably policemen, too!

"There were four radio cars," Moran went on, "and a couple of sedans full of detectives. I thought there'd been a murder or something. I was scared green."

That didn't sound like the police pursuit, Wentworth thought. Hell, the car that followed had been the ambulance! He was abruptly sure of that. He had not got a clear glimpse of the machine, but his memory brought back the outlines in the shadows. Yes, it had been the ambulance which followed! He started the Hispano again and spun across the city eastward.

"Where do we go now?" Moran wanted to know.

"We're going to find Jimmy," Wentworth called above the hiss and drumming of the wind, "and we've got to go fast if we're going to find him alive!"

The Hispano skidded half across the street on a turn, and the motor held a deeper note. "I've got a clue to the man behind this blind terror!"

CHAPTER 3
CHECKMATE

MORAN LEANED toward him and shouted questions above the car's roar, but Wentworth only shook his head. It was a fantastic thing he had conceived, but it was by no means impossible.

There was an Underworld character who had never come up against the law because he preyed on those who could not afford to go to the law for redress. The man was called Plantain, and his profession was hi-jacking and kidnaping crooks who would pay their ransom and be afraid to squawk. Often the victims didn't survive the kidnaping. These things Wentworth had learned through underground sources which he had established. Plantain was a name criminals whispered in a fear and dread almost equal to that which they felt for the Spider!

There were two things that pointed to the possibility of Plantain. The man had several times used the ambulance trick to seize victims; and it had been whispered that he had spied out the ground for several of his coups in the disguise of a blind

peddler, a beggar with a cane. This was the guise the leader of the Schultz bandits had assumed.

The Underworld knew little about Plantain except his deeds, but Wentworth had thought it well to investigate the man. Anyone of Plantain's intelligence might well become a wholesale menace, though Wentworth rather approved of his hostility to criminals. What Wentworth had learned was that he had, on the occasions of kidnaping, used ambulances of a sanitarium in Westchester called Oak Rest. It was toward the sanitarium Wentworth was racing now....

Wentworth stopped once. He picked the locks of Moran's handcuffs and went into a telephone booth where he got in touch with his fiancée, Nita van Sloan, the only woman who knew the secret of his double existence. He instructed her to take Linda into her protection and carry her to his penthouse on Fifth Avenue. Nita was to remain there also, as she invariably did when Wentworth was engaged in a major battle with the Underworld. His enemies had many times attempted to strike at him through the woman he loved. It was far wiser to place her in the armed fortress into which he had converted the entire building below his penthouse and which he had found expedient to buy.

Nita's voice was quiet as she accepted the command. "Is it— serious, Dick?" she asked.

"God knows," Wentworth replied. "You can see what a weapon for criminals this substance that causes blindness could become. And it looks as if Plantain were behind it. I'm on my way to the Oak Rest Sanitarium now." He laughed, a foreign note of tenderness in his voice. "Of course, I'll be careful, dear! See you for breakfast!"

A half minute later the Hispano was roaring along the roads to Westchester again.

The Oak Rest Sanitarium set well back from the road in the midst of a great grove of the trees from which it derived its name. A high stone wall whose top was encrusted with broken glass surrounded the grounds which were patrolled by watchmen and huge, savage dogs after dark. These facts alone would have been enough to arouse the suspicions of the Spider, even if he had not traced Plantain's ambulances to this source.

As they neared the sanitarium over the looping, narrow hill road, he rapidly explained these circumstances to Moran.

"Plantain is a hang-over from prohibition days," he finished, "and he would not hesitate to exterminate anyone who stood in his way. It is plain that Jimmy holds some secret which can damage Plantain. What that is, I do not know. It is possible that Jimmy does not know, either. But Plantain...."

His voice broke off as they crested a hill. He could see on the knoll beyond the valley the subdued lights of the sanitarium. Wentworth pulled into a wooded lane and got out. From the rear of the Hispano, he drew out two steel-shafted golf clubs with extra heavy heads. He handed one to Moran and balanced the other in his hand, smiling.

"I have found them effective against dogs on more than one occasion," he said simply. "The extra-long shaft comes in handy. It increases the reach, of course, and the force of the swing."

THUS ARMED, and with his automatics loaded again, he

led the way down the wooded slope toward the high wall surrounding the sanitarium. For a wide distance on each side of the stone barrier, trees and shrubs had been cleared away so that there were no overhanging branches which could be used as a ladder.

Moran braced his shoulders against the wall while Wentworth drew on thick driving gloves. Mounting Moran's shoulders, he picked a spot where the broken glass was short. He put his weight on his hands, winced as bits of glass cut through his gloves, and muscled himself erect on stiff arms. It was simple then to set a foot on the wall, and the glass could not penetrate shoe soles. He stooped and drew Moran up with the golf clubs. They jumped to the ground inside and stole softly through the trees, each ready with a club in hand.

Within a hundred yards of the building, Wentworth was beginning to hope that they would reach it without meeting any of the savage beasts. Then he caught the rasp of spurned gravel from the darkness behind him. He whirled just in time. Charging silently through the darkness was a dog whose shoulders were better than three feet from the ground and which weighed fully a hundred and fifty pounds. As he glimpsed the beast it sprang from the ground straight at Moran!

"Down, Moran!" Wentworth warned softly. He whirled the club head in a full two-handed swing, as if he were driving a golf ball from a spot just above Moran's shoulder. Moran dropped on the word and the club thudded against the dog's head. The dog went limp, head twisted violently to one side, but the impetus of the leap flung it against Wentworth's body, sprawling him on the ground. He was up instantly with the club poised, but no second blow was necessary.

Moran bent wonderingly over the animal. His face was white.

"The beast has tusks two inches long!" he whispered. "You crushed his skull!"

They reached the shadows beside the sanitarium building without further challenge. Wentworth stooped to try a basement window. It yielded after a few moments' work. He slid through first, easing Moran to the cement floor after him. Together, clubs left behind, they advanced across the vast basement. A minute gleam of a flashlight confirmed the Spider's memory of the lay-out and he found the stairs. Half way up, Wentworth paused.

The step beneath his foot had made a slight noise. Not a creak, it was something more like the click of an electrical switch! Even as the thought occurred to him and he attempted to leap backward, a blaze of light blasted at him from all sides. There was a solid thud, and Wentworth realized a barrier had fallen behind them.

They were trapped on the steps, between narrow walls, a door before and behind, mercilessly exposed by the glaring light. Wentworth whipped out an automatic and blasted a shot straight into the heart of the white ray that dazzled him from ahead. It had no effect other than a deafening roar.

When he could hear again, a man was talking. "Damned nice of you to pay me this impromptu visit, my friend. Would you have the kindness to give your guns to Moran? I'm sorry, but it is a rule of mine not to allow gentlemen I do not know to carry firearms in my house."

Wentworth laughed shortly. The sound was still on his lips when he spun about and struck Moran cleanly on the point of the jaw, sprawled him unconscious against the barrier at the foot of the steps.

"Now, then," Wentworth said pleasantly, balancing his automatics in his palms, "would you care to come and collect these weapons of mine?"

For a moment there was dead silence save for the harsh breathing of the unconscious Moran. Then the man behind the lights chuckled again.

"I'll come, if you like, my friend," he said, "but I warn you that if I come, you won't like it."

Wentworth's thin lips smiled. "Aren't you, perhaps, too sure that I won't like it?"

The trap was inescapable, he knew, unless the way out led someway through the agency of the man who spoke. No matter how he came, the Spider would be ready. He laughed again sardonically. He had helped Moran to escape from the police— and Moran was a member of the gang that had blinded Linda and others in the holdup at Schultz's. A damned clever actor, that boy!

THE LIGHTS blinked out with the abruptness of death. And while they still glowed red on the retina of his eyes, Wentworth jumped soundlessly to where Moran lay. He collided with a man, and struck with all the power of his body behind the blow.

25

The man fell, pole-axed, and Wentworth stooped in his place, found that Moran was being lifted. He helped with the task, moving on silent feet, heard a door click shut behind him and then instantly a machine gun began its chatter of death. But the sound was muted, plainly within the enclosure on the steps, and Wentworth felt the blood drain from his face. But for his instantaneous action, his keen analysis of events, his body would lie weltering on the steps now, literally cut in half by bullets!

Wentworth followed deliberately where the tug on the unconscious body of Moran led him. Somewhere in the darkness ahead, the other man who helped with the task grunted with laughter.

"Pretty cocky, that fellow in there! Reckon he's even cocky now!" he guffawed.

Wentworth echoed his laughter, heard the man curse, and knew the tone of his voice had betrayed him. Instantly, he dropped Moran and sprang toward the sound. His outreaching gun, swinging, struck something that crunched sickeningly. A man screamed, and Wentworth closed in and chopped down again with the barrel of the automatic. The man slumped down. Wentworth dropped with him as overhead lights clicked on. They did not have the brilliance of those others, but they were dazzling to a man whose eyes had once more become accustomed to pitch blackness. For an instant, Wentworth could see nothing at all. And then, his eyes clearing, he became aware of a man who crouched over a sub-machine gun, of a half dozen other men who ringed him around with leveled automatics.

The body of the man he had struck down was half between

him and the machine gun. Wentworth wasted no time in parley. His automatic spoke, and the machine gunner was straightened out of his crouch by the punch of forty-five caliber lead. He fell forward limply, scrambling on the floor. From the darkness, the cultured voice that had first challenged Wentworth spoke again.

"No, no, don't kill the mad dog with your guns," the voice said. "I can devise a much more interesting demise for him!"

As the man spoke, a stab of pain shot through Wentworth's body that made him gasp. His muscles writhed and knotted. His guns blasted without his bidding and without direction; he felt his senses reel. He knew what was happening to him but was helpless to escape the powerful electrical current, pulsing through the floor, which had been turned upon him! He could see the other men dimly and they, too, were tortured by the electricity.

Abruptly, the current ceased to harass Wentworth. He struggled to rise, to fight, but he was unable to move. A man sauntered from the darkness—a man in the crumpled clothes of a mendicant, whose eyes were shielded by the black glasses of a blind man, who tapped before him with a cane as he advanced. He was chuckling under his breath, as though he laughed to himself over some private joke. His cane twitched the automatics from beneath Wentworth's helpless hands, then he had poised the ferrule just above Wentworth's neck.

"How do you wish to be punished, my friend?" the man asked gently. "My cane can bring you the death of the hemlock which will paralyze your body and leave your brain alive for a while, or I can throw you into quivering convulsions which will last throughout your lifetime.

"Or"—he bent close—"I can merely blind you."

The cane touched Wentworth's neck.

"Which would you prefer?"

CHAPTER 4
THE DEATH IN LIFE

WENTWORTH FOUGHT for the control of his muscles. What he must attempt was virtually impossible, but it was his only chance. His arm lay outstretched near the Blind Man's leg. He must grip that leg and jerk it toward him so quickly that the man would be thrown backward before he could use whatever device was in the cane. He must do this without any premonitory tensing of his muscles, with the power of his arm alone....

"Gosh," moaned a boy's voice from the darkness, "what have you done to Mr. Wentworth?"

The cane leaped from Wentworth's neck. "Wentworth?" the blind man cried softly. *"Wentworth?* Now that is very interesting. I must ask a few questions of Wentworth before I touch him with my cane!"

Wentworth lifted his head. He knew that first voice, unmistakably. It was Jim, Jimmy Carroll who had been kidnaped under the very nose of the police. He could not see the boy, but he could hear him in the darkness, fighting against some one holding him.

"You big palooka!" he cried, his voice breaking. "You couldn't do this to me if Mr. Wentworth weren't dead!"

Wentworth stirred. The strength was coming back to his muscles now at last and he peered into the darkness toward the sound of the boy's voice. It was then that he saw the girl. She came forward into the ring of light with quick little steps.

"You promised me the boy wouldn't be hurt!" she cried, "and somebody's bloodied his nose, and—" She saw Wentworth, saw Hal Moran unconscious beside him, and ran forward, threw herself down on her knees.

"Hal," she cried. *"Hal!"*

She was very close to Wentworth and he could see that the creamy pallor of her skin was natural, that the rich red of her hair had never been dyed. She was slim and young and lovely amid this tawdry bunch of killers. This, he realized, was Sue Moran! This lovely girl had betrayed her temporary employers into the hands of the bandits and assisted them to blind five people for life.

Quick movement in the shadows caught his attention and he saw a man in a white-coated uniform hurry up to the Blind Man, lean over to whisper deferentially to him. Beneath the dark glasses, the Blind Man's face split in a wide grin.

"Boys," he said, "you deserve to hear about this. The little raid on the Chiquero Club turned out beautifully. The take was fifteen thousand dollars!"

One of he men holding an automatic on Wentworth laughed out loud. "Swell, chief Did they use the Darkener?"

The Blind Man's dark-glass covered eyes swung toward him.

29

"Yes, they used the Darkener," he said. "The damned fools! Pinkie lost his head and sprayed about twenty men and women guests."

The man laughed again. "What the hell? What's a few eyes between friends?"

Wentworth's lips tightened. So they called that dread fluid of the blinding spray the Darkener!

The Blind Man said patiently: "It isn't that I care about the eyes, or who lost them, but I gave orders not to use too much of the Darkener yet. We still haven't a large supply, and it's slow to make. You understand, William, that Pinkie disobeyed orders?"

Wentworth saw the grin instantly leave the man's face, saw it grow pasty. "Sure, Chief, sure," he mumbled.

"You didn't wish to defend his action, did you, William?"

"Hell, no, Chief!" The man's hands trembled.

If Sue Moran had heard any of the colloquy, she gave no sign of it. Hal was beginning to recover consciousness under her ministrations.

She shot a venomous glance at Wentworth, her soft young lips curled. Wentworth inspected her curiously, then he shrugged. Before this, women had gone off the deep end for men, women as lovely and fresh as Sue Moran... His strength had fully returned now, but he feigned continued weakness. There were five guns trained on him even with the machine gunner dead.

"Pinkie," said the Blind Man, chuckling, "will be here in a few moments."

AS HE spoke, a door opened somewhere and let in a thread of light. Feet shuffled forward across the basement. Wentworth supposed that Jimmy had been carried away or he would have said something further. It was clear that the Blind Man intended to mete out punishment to Pinkie, not for blinding a score of

innocent people, but for wasting a precious substance of the criminals.

The man called Pinkie was thrust forward into the circle of light. He was a youngster and his eyes, the twitching of his mouth, marked him plainly a user of narcotics. The color came and went pinkly in his cheeks.

"Geez, Chief," he whimpered. "I had to do it. There was a mug in the crowd tried to pull a rod, and the sprayer got stuck and I couldn't cut it off."

The Blind Man smiled pleasantly. He lunged out abruptly with the cane and the man screamed, clapped both hands to his eyes, danced in agony.

"I do hate to waste the Darkener," the Blind Man murmured. He faced his men. "This is a more quickly acting variety. You will see that in a few seconds his eyes are white."

Sue Moran had covered her eyes in horror, the men were pale and all save one had his eyes on the moaning Pinkie. It was Wentworth's chance and he took it with a celerity that seemed more than human.

He bounded from the floor and reached the one man who

was watching him with movements so swift they blurred. The man jerked up his sagging gun and Wentworth seized the wrist, darted under the arm and heaved upward. The man's voice rose in a scream of pure agony, his arm popped dully as the joint was burst apart and the gun came clear in Wentworth's hand.

A great shouting laugh poured from Wentworth's lips. He dropped to his knees and sent a shot smashing through the ceiling light. The first and second shots almost blended, and the second one sped before the light was fairly gone toward the spot where the Blind Man stood, his cane half lifted in attack.

Instantly, Wentworth flung himself flat on the floor, rolled quietly away from the spot where he had crouched to shoot. Guns spewed red flame into the darkness and by their flash, he could see that Hal Moran had seized Sue and dragged her flat on the floor. Of the Blind Man, he saw nothing and felt a savage joy thrill all through him. If only that bullet had sped true!

Wentworth got to his feet, and in a swift, crouching run, he circled toward where he judged the Blind Man was. He groped on the floor, seeking the body, seeking some clue to the man's fate. His fingers found the warm stickiness of blood, but of the man himself there was no trace.

Furiously, Wentworth sprang erect and raced across the basement toward the door through which Pinkie and his captors had entered. He found the door, but it was locked solidly. Hiding the gun behind his body to cover its flash he fired twice into the lock, wrenched the door open and found himself on a short flight of steps. He scrambled up them in a frenzy of haste and burst out into a wide main corridor of the sanitarium.

A white-coated attendant was hurrying along the hall-way toward him and Wentworth reached him in long bounds, ground the gun muzzle into his ribs.

"The boy!" Wentworth snapped out. "Where is the boy who was brought here tonight?"

The man nodded eagerly. "I'll show you!"

He hurried Wentworth to an elevator and sped to the top floor. Wentworth thrust the man ahead of him into another corridor, followed him to a door. The man stepped back, smiling.

"In there!" he said.

Wentworth's smile was stiff. "You don't mind going first, I hope?"

The man tried to hang back, then he shrugged his shoulders, opened the door. He sprang through and the door slapped shut behind him, but not before Wentworth sent a slug blasting through the narrowing crack. Wentworth cursed, as he wrenched at the knob, but the door was securely locked. He had been tricked, damn it! The man's reluctance had been intended to arouse his suspicions, to cause him to thrust the man through first....

A hard suspicion was pounding through his veins. A man clever enough to accomplish that was smart enough to be a leader. This must have been someone high in the councils of the Blind Man. Wentworth leveled his revolver at the lock, remembered he had only one, at most two shells left in the weapon, and hesitated.

THROUGHOUT THE entire building, alarm bells were clanging. Men ran shouting through the corridors below.

Outside, lights blazed in white radiance over the entire grounds. Wentworth ran to a window and saw an ambulance streaking for the gates, glimpsed a man's white face at a window in the rear. Quick as thought, his gun flung up and a bullet smashed the glass of the window, drove the face back out of sight. He might be wrong, he might be… But that face had been the lean, dour lines of the Blind Man!

There was a grim smile on Wentworth's lips. He had given away his whereabouts by that shot, but he had done worse than that if he had killed the Blind Man. For Wentworth needed the leader alive. He thumbed open the gate of the pistol and found the last cartridge had been fired.

The elevator door clanged open and two men gripping guns boiled out. They opened a wild fire. Wentworth dodged into a doorway, locked the door behind him and crossed the room in a bound. He was on the third floor and one story down was the roof of a porch. Without hesitation, he flung up the window, hung from the sill by his hands and dropped. He reeled backward, fell and rolled.

Guns banged above him and lead thudded into the roof nearby. He had just time to catch the gutter with his hands as he went off the edge of the porch roof, to swing under and land on the floor of the porch itself. Even his empty gun was gone now, and racing toward him from across the lawn were two of the giant Alsatian dogs. Wentworth whirled now, cleared the rail of the porch in a running hurdle and made for the window where he had left the golf clubs. He reached them just in time, whirled to face the dogs. Both were hurtling through the air toward him.

Frantically, Wentworth sprang to one side and his movement lessened the blow of the club. He caught one dog a glancing blow on the head. It was momentarily stunned, walking in a stiff-legged helpless circle, but the other struck the ground, wheeled instantly, and launched a new attack for Wentworth's throat. There was no time to whirl the club for a new blow. Wentworth slipped the stick through his hands and set his shoulders. Straight into the mouth of the leaping dog, he drove the handle of the club!

He went down under the impact of the leap, his shirt was ripped from his chest by its claws, but the dog writhed in a death convulsion on the ground, the handle buried in its throat. There was no time to jerk the club free and the other lay behind the second dog, standing on braced legs, gathering himself for a leap.

Wentworth now hurled himself bodily toward the dog and from his throat there roared a challenging note, half-growl, half-howl, in imitation of the beast's own battle snarl. The animal checked on the point of flinging itself into the air and Wentworth's full weight went into a swinging right hook to the jaw. It twisted the dogs head about, knocked him off balance and Wentworth chopped savagely at the back of the neck. The animal went down, quivering....

Wentworth darted along the side of the building toward the garages. In the nearest building he found a dark and empty ambulance. He leaped in the driver's seat, and moments later was roaring along the road toward the gate. Behind him, a machine gun hammered and smaller arms made spiteful coughing sounds. Wentworth's lips were twisted with anger at the necessity of fleeing, but to remain meant certain death. By his escape now he could help Jimmy Carroll. There must be a phone nearby where he could summon State Police....

He found the phone, but when State Police arrived, the sanitarium was deserted except for the bodies of the dead, and Wentworth made his way heavily homeward. There was still a chance, a barest chance... If the Blind Man had thought it necessary to kidnap Linda Carroll, she must know something damaging to them. He must, in some way, find out what that was and through it trap this criminal chieftain.

Wentworth slipped in the trade entrance of his building, took the service elevator to his penthouse. The door was heavily bolted as always, but at his ring, old Jenkyns, who had been butler to his father before him, swung wide the door.

"Glad to see you safely back, Master Dick," he said, a smile wreathing his wrinkled old face, but Wentworth thought dully that there was worry in the clear, blue eyes. He started to speak of it, but he was tired. It would wait.

"Miss Nita is here, sir," Jenkyns said. "She's in the music room."

As he walked swiftly along the hall, his heart lifting at thought of seeing Nita again, Wentworth's ears caught the faint, distant notes of the piano. They swelled as he approached, but there was a heaviness, a lack of spirit in the music. Trepidation gripped him. Nothing had gone wrong. It must not... He hurried into

36

the music room and Nita, with a glad cry, sprang up from the bench and ran into his arms.

WENTWORTH BENT to her lips and for a moment, Nita clung to him, then she leaned back, her violet eyes worried. "Dick, I didn't get Linda."

"What?"

Nita shook her head. "Kirkpatrick had ordered her held prisoner in a hotel and when I got there to offer to be responsible for her...."

"Kidnaped!" Wentworth jumped ahead of her words. "But, good Lord, why did Kirk order her held in a hotel?"

"I've asked myself the same thing about Kirk," Nita said slowly. "I don't know why he did such a foolish thing."

Wentworth left her side and strode across the room, wheeled back again. Twice within a few hours' time, Kirkpatrick had behaved in utter contradiction to his usual canny self. He had refused to see the boy who wanted protection for his sister; he had taken that sister after she had almost been kidnaped, to a hotel where she would be less well protected than in a cell. By heaven, if Wentworth did not know Kirkpatrick so well for the staunch and upright friend he had always proved himself....

"I don't understand," he said slowly, shaking his head.

Damn it, they had fought side by side through a score of battles with the Underworld, and Kirkpatrick's assiduous attention to duty could not be disputed. He shrugged, smiled at Nita.

"We can be sure there is some good explanation," he said. He strode toward her and realized presently that Jenkyns was standing stiffly at attention in the arched doorway that joined drawing and music rooms. "Yes, Jenkyns?"

Nita's hand rested lightly on Wentworth's arm, her eyes on his face. God knew this man of hers had trials enough in his almost religious protection of his people against criminal beasts of prey. Sometimes, there was in her a longing that he might desert this hard way, turn to the happiness together which they had surely earned through so many long months of struggle. But she knew that she would not have him shirk the task to which he had pledged his life. If he did that, he would be less than the man she loved. Her hand tightened on his arm and he covered it with his own.

"What is it, Jenkyns?" Wentworth prompted again.

Jenkyns' blue eyes, that were so much younger than his wrinkled face, now met Wentworth's gaze directly.

"It's Sue and Hal Moran, sir," he began.

"What? The Morans here?" Wentworth started forward.

Jenkyns shook his head heavily. "No, sir, it's not that. But Sue and Hal... That is, sir, they're kind of relatives of mine. My dead sister's children."

Wentworth stared at him and felt anger stir hotly within him. Damn it, the infamy of those two conspirators would break this old mans heart!

"My niece and nephew, sir. Hal's a fine boy and Sue... You must help them, sir. You've helped so many, Master Dick...."

Jenkyns' eyes had dropped. There was a weary sag to the shoulders that were always so erect. Wentworth said sharply, "But, damn it all, Jenkyns, I..." He closed his lips tightly. No use to torture Jenkyns with the things he knew about Hal and Sue Moran.

"They wouldn't do anything really wrong, sir," Jenkyns' voice, the dignified, deep voice that had been a part of Wentworth's life as far back as he could remember. "They might be a little wild, without a father or mother, the way they grew up. But nothing really wrong, Master Dick…."

Wentworth strode abruptly forward and clapped an affectionate hand on Jenkyns' shoulder. "Of course, Jenkyns," he said. "I'll help them. I'll do what I can…" He looked down, startled.

Old Jenkyns was on his knees, his master's hand pressed to withered lips. Wentworth's throat closed as he helped the man to his feet.

"You mustn't do things like that, Jenkyns," he said gently. "After all, we like to help our friends. Such an old friend as you…."

Jenkyns turned sharply away, his shoulders braced back stiffly. He fairly ran from their sight and Wentworth went to Nita, his face drawn and gray. "Sue Moran helped the bandits who blinded five people at Schultz's today," he said woodenly, "and Hal helped the leader of the bandits take me a prisoner…."

Nita smiled confidently up into his face, "You've helped so many…" she repeated.

CHAPTER 5
A VISIT FROM DEATH

A S ALWAYS when the emotional stress of his many battles became too much for him, Wentworth turned to music for release. His beloved Stradivarius sang far into the night, though Wentworth himself was scarcely aware that his bow picked out the strings. Gradually, he drew out the solitude of his music the decision which he had known impended. In the morning, he must face Kirkpatrick. If the things he feared were true, he must force a showdown.

The decision reached, he replaced his violin in its case and turned to find that Nita, sunk in the depths of a soft chair, had waited for him. His smile to her was weary, but at peace, and she rose swiftly.

"I sent Jenkyns to bed," she said gaily, "and we're going back and mess up his kitchen. I've been exploring and there's a baked ham!"

Wentworth laughed and put an arm about Nita's waist, but his laughter was not without hurt. Such moments as these were all he and Nita could garner from their love. How could the Spider marry and look forward to a home and children?

The police, however much he might help them in their endless warfare with crime, did not look upon the Spider as a benefactor. He was wanted on a score of homicide charges. Under that shadow of disgrace, Wentworth was far too honorable to think of marriage. He had fought against even the consolation such moments as these could afford. He had his enemies

40

to thank for them, the enemies who had tried to strike at him through his love.

His arm tightened about Nita's waist, and in the dim hallway they stopped for moments as long as heartbeats before they went on together. Nita chattered gaily, but Wentworth scarcely heard. There was a tightness in his throat, a stinging in his eyes. He never regretted the path he had chosen, the path of service to mankind, but sometimes the denial it meant was hard to bear....

He stopped abruptly in his advance down the hall. That stinging in his eyes... He snatched Nita up into his arms, whirled and raced back the way he had come. As he ran, he grabbed a cord that swung near the front door. Alarm bells burst upon the air, sounding in the room of each of his men and in the hallway fifteen floors below where armed guards were on duty.

"What is it, Dick?" Nita gasped as he pivoted into the drawing room and bounded across it toward the terrace. "Oh, Dick, what...."

"Did your eyes start burning there in the hall?" Wentworth asked harshly.

"Yes," Nita said hesitantly, "but—Dick, you mean... *The Blind Man!*"

Wentworth raised his voice in a shout. "Ram Singh! Jenkyns! Jackson! Protect your eyes! Cover them with wet pads and get out on the terrace!"

For all his haste, Wentworth let Nita down gently before he drew his guns. He crouched to one side of the wide French doors that opened on the terrace. He repeated his cry and through the drawing room raced a figure draped in white, hand to eyes. The

41

man, a turbaned Hindu, paused beside Wentworth, threw aside the pad. His hand went to a knife hilt at his girdle and teeth flashed amid the bushy beard that covered his face.

"*Wah!* Is there battle then, *sahib?*" The Hindu's strong, nasal voice was vibrant with excitement.

Wentworth shook his head. "I don't know. My eyes burned, Ram Singh."

The Sikh had bound his life to Wentworth's long ago in the Punjab when Wentworth had saved his family from massacre by a hostile clan. Now he crouched beside the man he called master, his great shoulders tense and waiting. He was a fighting man, and a warrior of warriors through more generations than he could count. The scent of battle was in his nostrils, and he was beside the master he idolized....

Jackson came swiftly through the drawing room, carrying Jenkyns in his arms.

"No damage, sir," he reported crisply. "Jenkyns fell and hit his head." As he spoke he was untying a bandage from his eyes, then stooping over Jenkyns, who already was beginning to stir...

Wentworth shifted impatiently. "Good work, Jackson, did you hear anything?"

"Nothing except the bell and your call, sir," Jackson reported. NITA CAME close. "Dick," she whispered. "Over on the service roof—quickly...."

"Ram Singh," Wentworth said softly. The name was scarcely uttered when the Sikh glided off into the darkness. For a moment, the white of his tunic and turban glimmered and then he was gone.

"Jackson, watch this door. Don't enter. Those fumes will blind you. Keep Jenkyns here."

He caught Nita's hand and stole off after Ram Singh. "I saw something move near the kitchen window," she whispered. They reached the brick wall which separated the terrace from the balance of the roof, peered over. They could make out the line of the penthouse against the sky glow, but at first that was all. Then a man screamed!

The cry cut short, gurgling, and a whispered Punjab oath rasped through the darkness, the night split wide open with gun flame. With a thrust of his arm, Wentworth spilled Nita beneath the protection of the wall and his heavy guns began a rhythmic blasting, left, right; left, right. He fired at gun flashes with the almost uncanny skill that years of practice, of absolute life-and-death dependence on those weapons, had given him. With the echo of his first shot, the volume of the attack decreased.

"Ram Singh!" he shouted, using the Sikh's native Punjabi tongue. "Capture one man alive!"

There was no reply, but the shadows against the base of the penthouse changed their outline a little. Wentworth's guns continued to leap in his hands. Hostile bullets thudded against the wall, sent brick dust burning into his face. He handed an empty gun to Nita.

"Fresh clips in my right hand pocket," he said quietly.

In a few seconds, he had the reloaded weapon in his hand, but the battle was practically over. One gun spurted at him twice more, then was silent. After slow, dark minutes dragged past, Ram Singh's voice came to Wentworth in a soft hail. Out of the night, the Sikh's white shadow loomed. He tossed a man's limp body over the wall, swarmed over after it.

"*Wah, sahib!*" he said harshly. "My knife drank only once. They were but mice who attacked the lion!"

Wentworth laughed and the sound was grim. "Bring your prisoner," he ordered. "Good work, Ram Singh. Jackson, you reconnoiter."

Jackson strode off across the terrace and Ram Singh struck a match above the face of his prisoner. A great oath caught in Wentworth's throat and Nita's hand touched his arm.

"What is it, Dick?" she whispered.

Wentworth laughed sharply. "This is one of those I promised Jenkyns I would help," he said harshly. "The prisoner is… *Hal Moran!*"

At his side, Jenkyns made an inarticulate sound. He went down on his knees by the unconscious man.

"Hal," he said. "Hal, why…."

Wentworth turned sharply away as Jackson came striding back through the darkness. "Three dead, sir," he reported quietly. "Two shot, one knifed. I think at least two others were wounded by bullets. They escaped by sliding down ropes to a lower apartment. Shall I follow?"

Wentworth shook his head. "The guards on the lower floors can do as much as you that way. Open as many windows as you can from the outside. Watch your eyes." He turned back to where Jenkyns knelt over the younger man's body. Moran was recovering consciousness.

His head rolled, his eyes fluttered. A word pushed at his lips.

He sat bolt upright with a cry, saying a girl's name, *"Linda!"* He stared wildly about him, sank back to the floor.

"Uncle Harold," he murmured, rolled his head and saw his captor. "Mr. Wentworth! You can't make me talk!" he cried. "I won't talk!"

Jenkyns twisted his hands. "Why, Hal," he whispered. "Why did you do such a thing as this?"

Lying there under the glare of the flashlight which Jackson held on him, Hal Moran seemed terribly young. His wavy brown hair was rumpled, his eyes were as guilty as a child's.

"I can't talk, Uncle Harold," he pleaded. "Don't try to make me, because I can't."

"Get up, Jenkyns," Wentworth ordered crisply.

The habit of obedience lifted the aged butler to his feet. He stood twisting his hands. "He is a good boy, Master Dick," he said humbly. "There is a reason for this. I know there is."

Wentworth pulled Moran to his feet. "I promised Jenkyns to help you," he said woodenly, "but I never yet have allowed a criminal to go unpunished. If you have an explanation...."

Hal Moran looked at the floor, "I can't talk," he said stubbornly.

Across the length of the drawing room, Wentworth saw the door that led to the public hall swing open.

"Be careful!" he shouted. "There's gas in here!"

HE SAW then that the men were police and that they wore gas masks. They stalked through the gloom of the drawing room like monsters out of a nightmare, and Wentworth recognized that the man who led them was his friend, the Commissioner of Police, Stanley Kirkpatrick. On the terrace, Kirkpatrick took off his mask, looked at it.

"Standard equipment these days," he said absently. "Came in handy. What happened, Dick?"

Wentworth explained briefly and Kirkpatrick looked grimly at Moran. "So he's Jenkyns' nephew, eh? Well, maybe our questioning will be more productive." He handed an officer his gas mask. "Take the prisoner to headquarters and find out what he knows."

Jenkyns' face was tortured but his eyes remained steady. "If I could have a gas mask, sir," he said humbly. "I'd like to go with him. Perhaps I can help. Hal isn't a bad boy at heart."

Kirkpatrick refused curtly and Wentworth studied him through narrowed eyes. It was queer that police arrived so promptly. He knew that his own men had not summoned them, and it was unlikely that shots fifteen stories above the street could be heard. The apartments of the building itself were thoroughly soundproofed... He recalled that police had been at the Moran apartment before there had been any shooting; that it was through Kirkpatrick's intervention that it had been possible for Linda to be kidnaped. His mobile lips tightened.

"Kirkpatrick," he said harshly, "I want to talk with you privately."

In the light that streamed out from the drawing room, turned on as the police led Moran away, the commissioner's face was pale and even more gaunt than usual. There were hollows beneath his eyes, sinks in his cheeks. Wentworth realized abruptly that Kirkpatrick looked old.

"Whatever you have to say," Kirkpatrick replied crisply, "can be said right here." There was irritation, almost anger in his tones.

Wentworth continued to stare at him, undecided. There was nothing in common between this irritable official and the Kirkpatrick who was his friend. For a moment, Wentworth had a wild suspicion that the real Kirkpatrick had been spirited away and an impostor substituted. But at once he recognized the impossibility of that.

Any man as familiar as the Spider with the art of disguise would know at once of any such subterfuge. But Kirkpatrick had changed… With that realization, Wentworth knew a sharp recurrence of his suspicion. The Kirkpatrick he had known would not have conspired with criminals, as the Spider increasingly feared the commissioner had. But would this changed, this altered Kirkpatrick….

"All right," Wentworth said slowly, "I'll say it here. Would you mind telling me why Linda Carroll was placed in a hotel from which it was easy for her to be kidnaped, instead of in jail where she normally would have been put?"

Kirkpatrick took an angry stride forward. "Are you implying that I did that deliberately, to help…."

Wentworth met his glare directly. "An attempt has been made previously to kidnap Linda Carroll," he said, "which I understand the Spider prevented. I know that she asked to be put in jail. Yet you placed her where it would be a simple matter for the Blind Man to reach her. I would like to know why."

Kirkpatrick's fist clenched. "Damn you, Wentworth," he cried violently. "If I didn't…."

He started forward, stumbled and lifted a clenched fist to his forehead. He swayed and Wentworth put out a hand to steady him. Kirkpatrick struck it aside, glared at him.

Heavy footsteps pounded across the drawing room and both men swung that way. The policeman running toward them whipped off his mask as he got clear of the contaminated air, stood stiffly at salute.

"Commissioner," he gasped. "Commissioner, the—the prisoner escaped from us!"

Wentworth took an angry stride forward, his fists clenched. "Without help," he said, deeply, "that man escaped from the police?"

"Yes, sir," the policeman stammered, flinching. "He broke away and slid down the dumbwaiter cable. We shot at him, but…."

Wentworth threw back his head and laughed harshly, then swung to face Kirkpatrick. "You don't want to explain that either, do you, Kirkpatrick?" He leaned close and said in a low, restrained voice, "You can't explain it by anything except that you—*you are in league with the Blind Man!*"

CHAPTER 6
BLIND MEN

THE INSTANT Wentworth had made that accusation, he regretted it. Not that there wasn't evidence enough to

48

arouse suspicion, but he and Kirkpatrick were friends, closer friends than most people would have believed possible, each ordinarily ready to die in the others stead. However, this was no matter of friendship. The people whom Wentworth defended had been attacked... Kirkpatrick had never swerved in a choice between duty and friendship. Why should Wentworth swerve now from his plain course for friendship's sake?

Yet this very integrity which was one of Kirkpatrick's outstanding characteristics should gainsay such an accusation as Wentworth had made. Kirkpatrick throw in with criminals? It was unthinkable. There was some other explanation... There *had* to be!

Wentworth laughed, "Forgive me, Kirk. I'm nervous, over-wrought, I guess. I don't, of course, believe you are in league with criminals."

Kirkpatrick stared at him through long moments, then pivoted on his heel and stalked across the drawing room, ignoring the danger of the gas that blinded. Apparently, it had been fully dissipated by the circulation of air, for he suffered no ill effects. Wentworth stood motionless, watching him go, the hand he had offered dropping to his side.

Nita came slowly to Wentworth's side and they stood together silently.

"I was precipitate in accusing him, of course," Wentworth said softly. "But, damn it, he has accused me on much less evidence of being the Spider... And he seems so different from the old Kirk we used to know. I wish to God I knew what his game was!"

Sleep was long in coming when finally the police had gone and Wentworth retired to his quarters. But his awakening was more awful than his sleep-time thoughts.

The morning brought him news that seven times during the night the Blind Man had struck, and in each case a man of leading position in industry or capital had been terribly blinded. In four cases, members of the victim's family or his servants had attempted to balk the criminals and been blinded also. In all, the toll of the night's horror was thirteen!

Wrath stirred in Wentworth's soul, and his thoughts flew again to his accusation of Kirkpatrick. God above, how could the Kirkpatrick he knew be guilty of allying himself with the devils who committed such atrocities! But, he considered, Kirkpatrick was not the man he had known. Something had changed him—unbelievably. Wentworth calmed himself with an effort and went about the preparation for the day. Nita shared his breakfast, but he was silent, engrossed in analysis. He could discover no reason for the attack on the seven men the night before.

In no case had anything been stolen, or tampered with. There had been no effort to intimidate the men before the blinding took place. Wentworth looked up sharply, and the glimpse of Jenkyns' downcast face softened his voice.

"Have Jackson check up on the men who were blinded last night," he instructed, "and see if they are connected in any business way. And Jenkyns...."

The butler turned at the door and waited silently. "Don't worry too much about Hal and Sue," Wentworth admonished. "If, as you say, they are innocent, I'll see to it that they don't suffer."

A smile trembled on Jenkyns' lips. "Thank you, Master Dick, but I am no longer sure." He turned heavily away, but Wentworth stopped him.

"A minute, Jenkyns," he said. "This is a curious situation and I have an idea that… Jenkyns, if the Blind Man asks you to betray me, appear to fall in with his plans."

"But, Master Dick!"

Wentworth smiled. "I have a reason for asking it!"

Jenkyns bowed, the lines of trouble and anxiety clearly imprinted on his features. Wentworth turned to Nita. "You'll have to reassure Jenkyns for me, dear, about those children he loves," he said. "If those two can be saved, I'll save them. Jenkyns has never been censorious of my activities, except to worry over my being hurt. Certainly, I can't be less than helpful to those he loves."

Nita leaned forward, "Even if they prove to be close allies of the Blind Man? Even if they have blinded people—killed them?"

Wentworth's eyes narrowed a little, and Nita nodded. "No, I can't reassure Jenkyns more than you have done. He *knows* you'll be just. But he wants more than that."

Wentworth was silent through the rest of the meal and there was a frown in his usually clear gray-blue eyes. Certainly the way he traveled was painful, since it might lead him to destroy the loved ones of a man devoted to him, or to battle with the man who had been his friend and staunch companion in a score of deadly fights. When the meal was finally finished, Jackson was waiting to make his report.

Not only were the seven blinded men connected more or less directly, but the night club robbed the night before and Schultz's grocery were controlled by the man whom they served, one Walter Smythe, a Wall Street broker.

Two possibilities flashed instantly before Wentworth's mind:

Smythe was beset by a clever enemy or rival; or he was looting his own companies deliberately and destroying men who might block or expose him. Both had happened within Wentworth's experience. His lips set grimly as he rang for Jackson and the Daimler town car.

Walter Smythe would receive an early call this morning....

THE ENTRANCE to Walter Smythe's brokerage office was a hall all in rich gray as wide as a drawing room. The single window was a stained glass reproduction of a stock ticker with sprawling tape and the rampant symbols of bear and bull. In a far corner of the gray room there was a desk and chair, no other furniture at all.

The girl receptionist rose and came forward alertly, smiled when she recognized Wentworth. She had never seen him before, but it was her job to know the wealthy and prominent of the city. She greeted him by name, and ushered him into Smythe's office after only a momentary hesitation at the phone. She was a gay, golden little thing, as delightful as sunlight. She called Smythe "Dad."

Wentworth smiled after her as she left. "Your daughter?" he asked.

Smythe was a small dour man with eyebrows and mustache looking like three dabs of black in his pasty white features.

He managed a smile. "She insists on helping down here, but she slips up sometimes with that 'Dad.' People will think I can't afford to hire a reception clerk...."

Wentworth said gravely: "They'll be almost right if this Blind Man isn't caught soon, won't they?"

Smythe slapped the desk. "That remark was uncalled for," he said sharply. "I'll—have to ask you to state your business!"

Wentworth selected a chair and dropped into it, crossed his gloved hands over the head of his cane.

"Certainly," he agreed. "First, do you know of any enemy ruthless enough to have done what has been done to you in the last twenty-four hours?"

"You're speaking for the police?" Smythe demanded sharply.

Wentworth shook his head, smiling. Smythe nodded and dropped back in his chair. "I must apologize," he muttered, "the thing has me crazy."

"But do you have any idea who could hate you so much?" Wentworth persisted.

Smythe shook his head. "Cranks, of course, who have lost money, but they hardly come in the class with the Blind Man. They're the only persons I can think of, and I can't recall a single one by name."

Wentworth studied the dour little man steadily through a long silence, then he nodded sharply and got to his feet. If Smythe had readily named an enemy or two, he would have been inclined to suspect the man, but as it was… He stiffened suddenly.

The scream from the front of the offices was shrill and awful in its intensity, a voice of a woman in unbearable pain.

Smythe whipped about his desk, but Wentworth was before him at the door. He sprang through, gun in hand.

Toward them down the hall staggered the gay little golden girl, her hands covering her eyes and her agonized screams soaring on and on. Wentworth darted past while Smythe threw his arms about her and instantly Wentworth's guns began to speak.

There were five men in the gray room with its window of stained glass. Two in front held narrow hoses in their hands, leading to tanks upon their backs. The others had guns in their hands and all wore masks that protected their eyes.

Wentworth flung himself belly-down on the floor. Lead whined past his head, gouged up the gray rug beside his arm. The glass door of an office smashed and spray from one of the hoses licked out—and then it was all over. Five swift, rhythmic shots from his two guns and Wentworth was on his feet again. In the gray foyer, there was puddles of red and the five men had almost ceased to writhe.

"Stay out of the foyer!" Wentworth shouted clearly. "Stay out or you'll go blind!"

He hurried Smythe and the girl back into his office and closed the door against the damnable vapor. Smythe's daughter had ceased to scream, but she still breathed in long, exhausted sighs. As Wentworth faced them, Smythe in terror dragged down the girl's hands from her face and his wild curse almost drowned her renewed scream.

Her eyes that had been blue and smiling were gone. From their pits two white, opaque balls stared sightlessly.

SMYTHE WHIRLED to Wentworth. "I wouldn't talk before because they threatened my daughter, but I will now. Nothing else matters. The Cyrils have been blackmailing me for years and when they'd milked me dry they set out to ruin me. The father is a blind inventor who claims I stole an invention of his and has got forged proof that I'm afraid to fight. If my reputation were once attacked…."

"I see," Wentworth said, "and where can I find these Cyrils?" His voice was quiet, but there was a sickness and a pain within him. That lovely, golden girl….

Smythe held the girl tightly in his arms and muttered an address on the lower East Side. Wentworth left and drove northward toward the Cyril's address.

It seemed queer that, if they had bled Smythe white as he charged, they should occupy quarters in so poor a neighborhood. He shook his head. The truth was, probably, that Smythe was wild with grief and ready to accuse anyone.

Jackson, who was driving him, slid the Daimler town car to a halt and Wentworth, looking out, realized with a start that the apartment house in which the Cyrils lived was the same Linda Carroll occupied.

Rapidly, Wentworth entered the building, took the elevator to the fifth floor where, the directory stated, the Cyrils had apartment 5-F.

His knock at the door brought no response through long minutes, then it opened a little way on a stout chain and through the crack wild black eyes peered out at him.

"What do you want?" the man demanded harshly.

Wentworth deliberately drew a wallet from his pocket and fingered out money. "Smythe sent me," he said.

The door closed, opened again without the chain and Wentworth entered. The man who had peered at him was narrow-faced, stooped, apparently the son Smythe had mentioned. His fingers were stained with chemicals and he wore an acid-scored rubber apron. Black hair scrambled wildly down over his pale, scowling forehead.

"Well, pay up and get out!" he ordered roughly.

Wentworth shook his head. "I'll have to see your father first." He was studying the man keenly. Unless he were totally unable to judge character, this man had the potentialities of a dangerous criminal, but not of the type against which he was fighting. This man was no leader. His crime would be of the furtive kind, murder in the night, or dynamiting.

Young Cyril reluctantly led the way into a room whose entire side was windows. Against them was a long laboratory bench and before it, perched on a high stool, was a bent and white old man.

"What is it, Francis?" the man asked quietly. His voice was gentle and his face, turning toward Wentworth, was kind. The eyes were sightless. Wentworth shook his head. Smythe was wrong if he suspected these two. The son might blackmail him, yes, but there the crime stopped.

Wentworth laughed. "I just came to look at you, Mr. Cyril. Walter Smythe seemed to think you might be responsible for some of the new crimes, but I can see at a glance that you are not. Thank you for letting me come in." He handed the money to the younger Cyril, who snatched it ungraciously. He had his hand on the doorknob ready to leave when a fist beat thunderously outside.

"Open in the name of the law!" a man shouted. "Open before we smash the door in!"

CHAPTER 7
AGAINST THE LAW

THE FIRST word of the police outside brought a gun leaping to the hand of the younger Cyril. He leveled it at the door and only Wentworth's prompt leap prevented him from firing through the wooden panel.

"You fool!" Wentworth cried sharply. "They'd burn you for that!"

The man was on him in a fury, striking with wild fists. "I knew you were just a spy for Smythe! It's a trap!" he shouted. "Damn you, I'll kill you!"

Wentworth twisted Cyril's arms behind him, carried him back to the laboratory. "Police are at the door," he explained rapidly to the old man who met him there. "I don't know what they want you for, but it's my guess that Smythe has sworn out some charge. Do you want to surrender, or shall I help you to escape?"

The old man smiled gently. "Why, we will surrender," he said calmly. "We have done nothing for which the law should reproach us."

"That's wise," Wentworth assured him. "I'll see that you don't suffer. My name is Wentworth—Richard Wentworth. You can call on me." He thrust the gun he had taken from the younger man into a pocket, went to the door.

"All right!" he called. "This is Wentworth. I'll open the door."

The police trooped in, rather subdued in Wentworth's presence.

As Wentworth had guessed, it was a warrant sworn out by Smythe charging mayhem and attempted robbery of his office through agents. The elder Cyril accepted it without demur, but his son flew into a rage that bordered on insanity. He shouted and waved his hands furiously in the air until he was handcuffed.

Wentworth journeyed with the Cyrils to police headquarters and saw that they had a lawyer, then he sought again the trail of Smythe's enemies. It seemed fairly obvious that some powerful, hidden enemy wanted to destroy Smythe....

Wentworth's search was fruitless, and late in the afternoon he returned to his penthouse and Nita. She met him at the door, her smile eager and excited.

"Linda Carroll is here!" she cried. "Hal Moran helped her to escape and she came straight to you!"

His hopes rising, Wentworth strode briskly to the room to which Nita had assigned the girl. Linda turned her blind face hesitantly toward the door as he entered. Her affliction subdued her voice. She only murmured his name inquiringly.

Wentworth put a hand on her shoulder. "Yes, Linda. And I'm glad you got away from the Blind Man."

A shudder trembled over her slender body. "I don't think I shall ever really get away from him. It's awful, the darkness... I found a taxi and told the man to bring me to you. I couldn't know whether he was coming here or not. You are—very kind."

She was silent for a while, then she lifted her face. It was pitiful, the lifting of those white, sightless eyes. "I hope I have some information which may repay you a little," she said. "The Blind Man is going to rob some theaters tonight...."

A sharp curse escaped Wentworth, but he urged the girl to go on.

"I don't know much more than that," Linda said faintly. "I don't think he plans to rob the people, just the box office safes. He didn't say what theaters, I only understood that he meant to rob more than one. That's all. I hope it will help."

"It will!" Wentworth assured her. "It will. Miss van Sloan says that Hal helped you...?"

"Oh, he was wonderful!" Linda cried softly. "The Blind Man made him go out with some men last night, and held me as hostage. If Hal hadn't have come back to get me... But he did, and this afternoon when they were all resting, he found me and took me to the street. Then he went back to the Blind Man! I couldn't keep him from it. I couldn't... in the dark. He went back for Sue. Oh, he's a good boy, Mr. Wentworth! You must save him if you can. I know it's asking a lot, but he is a good boy...."

WENTWORTH PATTED her shoulder reassuringly. "You love him, Linda."

"Oh, yes!"

Wentworth stared unseeingly through the window at the deepening dusk. The fact of Linda being held hostage for him would explain Hal's refusal to talk and also his escape, but it was still strange that the Blind Man would have sent him on the task. Surely, with the weapon he possessed, the Blind Man did not need to draft unwilling men by such methods as that!

"Do you know where you were, Linda, when you got in the taxi?" Wentworth asked.

"Where Fordham Road and Grand Concourse intersect,"

HAL MORAN

SUE MORAN

WALTER SMYTHE

Nita put in quietly. "I found the taxi driver and checked back."

"Had you walked far then?" Wentworth turned to Linda.

"I can't tell you," Linda said in her small voice. "My... my blindness is so recent...."

"That's all right," Wentworth assured her. "You've helped me a great deal. Perhaps, before morning, we'll have the Blind Man captive and be able to free your Hal!"

"Oh, I shall pray to God for that!" Linda cried, turning her white, pitiful eyes to his face again:

Wentworth strode out of the room, his forehead knotted in a frown. Those poor eyes! God, it wouldn't be enough to find and kill the Blind Man!

If there were any cure possible for these poor blinded victims, he would wring it from the Blind Man—by torture, if necessary.

Nita joined him presently on the terrace where he paced anxiously back and forth. The August dusk meant that already it was well past eight o'clock, and the bandits undoubtedly would strike shortly after nine. And, suspicious as he was of Kirkpatrick, how could he trust to the police to foil the attempt? It would be futile for the Spider alone to try to guard the theaters. More than one would be attacked and, regardless of his skill and genius, he could not hope to defend them all....

LINDA CARROLL

THE BLIND MAN

JENKYNS

"I'll have to go to Kirkpatrick," Wentworth told Nita. "There is no other way. If Kirkpatrick doesn't take the proper action…."

Nita gazed deeply into his eyes and there was a touch of dread in her own gaze at what she saw. Dick could rise so above human emotion; he could crush his greatest friend rather than allow the criminals to succeed in their frightfulness… She went close to him and laid her hands upon his chest.

"I'm—afraid, Dick," she whispered.

Wentworth's arms circled her, his lips brushed the soft sweetness of her mouth.

"I'll need Ram Singh and Jackson with me," he said briefly then. "See that everything here is locked up tightly—and you'd better get out a sub-machine gun…."

Nita nodded to the swift rush of words, but her eyes still clung to his. "Dick," she whispered, moving back to him "Dick, Kirkpatrick has been your friend through many years. Don't be too quick in your judgment. There must be some explanation for his strange actions. Someone may be driving him mad, or perhaps have a hostage against him."

Wentworth shook his head. "He would never budge for that. I've been held prisoner by criminals, and so has his nephew, Corcoran, but Kirk would have seen us both dead rather than let our safety influence his actions. They wouldn't succeed any better now."

"But if he is sick?" Nita urged. "If someone is drugging him…."

"Then he must be removed from a position where he can harm people!" Wentworth said calmly. "Don't worry, sweetheart." He kissed her gently. "I must go. Don't forget to lock things tight—don't forget the machine gun…."

He turned toward the drawing room entrance and saw Linda Carroll leaning a hand against the door jamb. "I… I couldn't stay in the room," she whispered. "It was crushing me."

WENTWORTH EYED her for a moment, then strode on and left her with Nita. But while the Daimler, with Jackson and Ram Singh in the front seat, zigzagged toward police headquarters, his thoughts were still on the girl. He had accepted into his home one who had been in the power of the enemy, whose loved ones still were hostages. Hal Moran and her brother, Jimmy. Though blind, she had made her way to a point where she could overhear a fragment of his plans… It seemed mad to suspect Linda, but Wentworth had met treachery too many times to overlook such a possibility. A block from police headquarters, he stopped the car and telephoned Nita.

"Don't let Linda use a phone or communicate with anyone," he warned. "I'm inclined to trust her, but we can't be sure. She overheard my plans, such as they are."

Nita assented and Wentworth pushed on to headquarters.

Never before had he had the least difficulty in reaching Kirkpatrick, but now he was compelled to wait in the big main room downstairs through long minutes. He forced himself to patience, and presently he was ushered up the stairs. Seated behind his desk, in the great square room that was his office, Kirkpatrick did not rise to greet his friend.

"Well," he demanded harshly, "what do you want?"

More clearly than any of the things that had happened between them, his present manner indicated how far apart they had grown. Anger sprang into Wentworth's brain, but he thrust it down. He had come tonight, not for himself, but for the safety of all the hundreds who were at the theaters. True, the bandits' plans called for looting only the safes—however, the Blind Man would make sure of his thefts by using the blinding Darkener. He was callous of human misery and life….

Wentworth walked quietly forward until he stood against Kirkpatrick's desk. His eyes burned into those of his friend, scanned the gaunt sunken lines of his saturnine face. Nita had been right. There was misery here. Wentworth held out a hand, palm upward.

"Kirk," he said, "I want to apologize for what I said the other night. If you won't accept that, at least let us forget our quarrel until we have beaten the Blind Man. Together, we can accomplish almost anything, but separate…."

Kirkpatrick reared back in his chair, his face twisted into lines of bitterness.

"There can be no union between you and me, Wentworth," he said harshly. "You are outside the law."

It would have been a little funny, that declaration, if there were not such stark agony in the depths of Kirkpatrick's blue eyes. Kirkpatrick had known for years that Wentworth was the Spider; convinced of it, but unable to prove it.

"I approve of this Spider's work," he had once told Wentworth, smiling sardonically. "He's a great help, but he's also a murderer. I hope the evidence of your guilt never falls into my hands, Dick, for if it does, I shall prosecute you to the full limit of my strength and ability!" There could be no doubt that he had meant precisely that.

Wentworth said softly:

"All right, I'm outside the law. Now we'll see how firm is *your* allegiance to the law. I have information that the Blind Man will rob several theaters tonight. What are you going to do about it?"

Kirkpatrick looked directly into Wentworth's eyes. His lips twitched as he pressed a button on his desk. For moments nothing happened, then the door flung open behind Wentworth and feet rushed forward. Too late he sensed treachery and whirled. Men in the uniforms of police, with the faces of criminals, ringed him with drawn guns!

"Nice work, Kirkpatrick," snarled the man who obviously was the leader of the gunmen. "All right, boys, give it to him! The boss said not to give him a single chance this time."

The man lifted up his heavy police revolver and pointed it directly at Wentworth's heart!

CHAPTER 8
FRIEND OR TRAITOR?

THERE WERE four men with guns trained on Wentworth at a range at which a novice would have difficulty in missing. And these men were far from novices, either at guns or killing. Behind Wentworth, was the man who had summoned these wolves to the kill, his friend, Kirkpatrick!

Wentworth's body was totally relaxed. There was even a slight smile on his lips. He said calmly: "I take it that your boss is the Blind Man?"

The leader with the gun said: "That's right, bo. Where would you rather have it, heart or head?"

"Oh, the head decidedly," Wentworth told him pleasantly. "I always shoot in the head myself. It kills instantly, and it paralyzes, too, so that the man can't shoot back. For instance...."

Wentworth's hands moved with blurring speed as he ducked sideways and down. As he talked, the guns of the killers had shifted almost automatically toward his head, and the mingled crash of the four weapons sent their lead at the spot where his head had been. Before they could fire again, Wentworth's own guns were in action. The leader's feet lifted from the floor and his body, already dead, thumped against a second man, spilling both. Wentworth blew another man against the wall with a bullet and then... His foot slipped.

A faint despairing cry flew from Wentworth's lips. He had known that sometime in the midst of frantic action, his keenly attuned body would fail him. He would move too slowly, or his aim would err. It was inevitable for a man who fought so often at such desperate odds. Off balance, he dropped one gun, tried to catch himself with that hand while he brought the second weapon into play. One of his remaining enemies was sprawling on the floor, under the body of a dead companion, but the fourth man was ready. He was standing, flat-footed, a thin grin on his mouth, his automatic swinging in a short deadly arc. He could not miss, could not….

Wentworth flung a crazy shot at him and the man did not even move. Wentworth's one hand twisted his body as he hit the floor. He rolled on his back, trying to bring his gun to bear and saw the automatic of the killer steady on his head. Yes, this was death. Even while he fought frantically to overcome the momentum and impact of his fall, to bring his gun into line, Wentworth recognized that he would fail.

A grim smile twisted his lips; the crash of the gun was thunderous. Wentworth's body twitched and his own automatic spoke in reply. His eyes were on the man and he realized with a sense of shock that the gun in the man's hand had not moved, that the shot he had expected to end his life had not been fired….

Wentworth was instantly on his feet, crouching over his automatic. He took a long stride forward and slugged the one living man, stared again at the killer who had almost slain him. The man was twisting slowly on feet that had no grip on the floor. His face, scowling, rage-twisted, turned to Kirkpatrick. Amazement sponged his countenance and he went to the floor all at once, a lax heap.

Kirkpatrick was standing behind his desk, smiling bitterly

down at the long-barreled revolver in his hand. He tossed it into his drawer as Wentworth strode toward him, sank into his chair as if all his strength had gone out of him. He lifted his long, powerful hands and pressed them into his temples, looking into Wentworth's eyes.

"The damned fool was going to kill you, Dick," he said.

Wentworth clapped a hand on Kirkpatrick's shoulder. He was laughing, and there was a stinging in his eyes.

"By God, Kirk," he whispered. "By God…" It wasn't that he had been so near death. That had happened a dozen times before. But Kirkpatrick had come through. At the last possible nick of time, Kirkpatrick had come through. He was himself again and now, together, they would win!

Kirkpatrick looked up into Wentworth's face and fear crept into his eyes.

"Dick," he whispered. "Dick, for God's sake, kill me, before… before…."

WENTWORTH STARED into the distraught face of his friend—and the alarm bells, the shouts and running of policemen through the building faded into nothingness. His fingers bit deep into Kirkpatrick's shoulder.

"What is it, old man?" he asked, swiftly. "Tell me! What hold have these crooks got over you? What are they doing to you?"

For a moment, something struggled up through the depths of fear in Kirkpatrick's eyes, his lips opened… The door crashed in and policemen with drawn guns stood staring wildly about the room.

"Someone disguised as police made an attempt on your

commissioner's life," Wentworth told them calmly. "I think one of them is only stunned. Take them away and Mr. Kirkpatrick will be down to question them shortly."

Kirkpatrick gestured assent and the police hurriedly dragged the bodies of the dead from the office, closed the door. Wentworth turned back to his friend and knew that the moment when Kirkpatrick might have spoken was gone. A heaviness settled about his heart. What dark secret was causing that strange change over the police commissioner? Whatever it was, Wentworth knew he must force it out in the open.

"Kirkpatrick," he said harshly. "There's no time to be lost. We've got to throw police guards around those theaters, warn their managements…."

He stopped, seeing the hardness creep into Kirkpatrick's jaw. "Man! You can't refuse!"

Kirkpatrick shook his head slowly, staring into Wentworth's eyes. "I can't act on your say-so. You'll have to tell me the source of your information."

Wentworth's lips set harshly. Kirkpatrick was within his rights, of course, but never before had he hesitated for a moment to act on the Spider's information. And Wentworth could not reveal that he had the tip from Linda….

He went cold for a moment, remembering that he had suspected Linda of being a spy for the crooks. Why, then, did he think that she had told the truth about this other matter?

Wentworth frowned. Linda would be an unwilling spy at best, forced to betray her friends through fear of what the Blind Man would do to her loved ones. No, she had told the truth about the theaters. And if he told Kirkpatrick the girl had brought him the information it would seal the girl's doom and that of the hostages the Blind Man held.

The thought tightened Wentworth's throat, narrowed his eyes. This man, his friend, the commissioner of police on whom the people depended for protection, would betray that innocent girl. In God's name, what hold did the Blind Man have over Kirkpatrick?

Wentworth started as he realized that he had phrased the thought out loud. Kirkpatrick was still facing him, a faint smile on his lips. Well, his course was plain wasn't it? Kirkpatrick seemed almost to invite it.

Wentworth stepped in swiftly, brought up his right in a clean blow. Kirkpatrick leaned into it deliberately. His head wrenched back and he crumpled into Wentworth's arms!

It was the work of an instant to handcuff Kirkpatrick with his own implements. Wentworth put him in a chair, locked the office door and sprang to Kirkpatrick's desk, slapped a dog on the annunciator that communicated with all the police offices.

Strangely, as he began to talk, it was not his own voice, but the clipped, metallic accents of Kirkpatrick which issued from his throat. He had worked too closely with Kirkpatrick in the past not to know which men he used on such occasions as these, how he arranged his forces.

Orders snapped out in swift succession with scarcely a pause for breath. Within five minutes, every theater in the city would be covered by a full squad of police with gas masks. They had orders to shoot to kill.

When that was done, Wentworth crossed to where Kirkpatrick still lolled laxly in the chair. There was grief in his face. He had no way of telling what injury the things he had just done would inflict on his friend; what hold the Blind Man had. His mouth shut grimly. Well, the Spider had never counted the cost even when that cost might mean the loss of the one woman in the world he loved. Why should he hesitate now? He stood on braced feet, massaged Kirkpatrick's neck and slapped him back to consciousness. Just as Kirkpatrick was beginning to stir, Wentworth leaned over him.

"Is it Corcoran, they've got prisoner?" he asked.

Kirkpatrick groaned. "Yes, and his wife and—the child."

A GREAT oath rasped from Wentworth's throat. Kirkpatrick's only nephew, the boy who had been like a son to him, that exquisite girl he had married, and three-year old baby! There was an unwonted tenderness in Wentworth's touch as he helped Kirkpatrick to his feet. He took off the handcuffs, gave him the commissioner's hat and urged him, still half-dazed, toward the door. However much he might pity his friend, he could not waver in his purpose. Precious though those three lives were, they could not be put into the balance against the thousands who would suffer from the Blind Man's depredations, if the police did not take vigorous action. He shook his head. It was strange, too, that Kirkpatrick should yield even to the threat of killing the three he loved most. But Kirkpatrick was not in a normal frame of mind. He was being torn by more than mental strife… Wentworth's eyes narrowed. Nita had suggested drugs. Tonight, he would see….

No one interfered as he and Kirkpatrick walked together through the halls of the police headquarters to the street. They entered Kirkpatrick's car and Wentworth signaled Ram Singh and Jackson to follow in the Daimler. A half dozen blocks away on a dark side street, Kirkpatrick was shifted, a prisoner, to Wentworth's car under Ram Singh's care and the handcuffs were replaced.

"I hate to do this to you, Kirk," Wentworth said heavily, "but there's no other way. I've got to find out what's wrong with you. Something is, you know. Not even the fact that Corcoran and the others were being held as hostages would have influenced you a few months ago. You must be drugged or something…."

Kirkpatrick leaned forward, staring into Wentworth's face as though the suggestion found a response in his own consciousness. "You may be right, Dick," he said. "But God, to think of Corcoran—the baby…" He buried his face in his shackled hands.

Wentworth rested a hand on his friend's shoulders—then he was gone.

"To the apartment, Ram Singh," he ordered. "His life and the *missie sahib's* be on thy head!"

"On my head be it, *sahib*," affirmed Ram Singh. The Sikh salaamed, lifting cupped hands to his turbaned forehead. Then he sprang to the driver's seat, and the car sped away. Wentworth, with Jackson beside him, strode to Kirkpatrick's car, parked around the corner with its police driver.

"He'll be curious about Kirkpatrick's not returning," Wentworth said slowly. "Slip up on him and knock him out."

He stood motionless in the shadows while Jackson stole quietly to the rear of the police limousine, paused, and then crept stealthily around to the driver's seat.

Wentworth's forehead was creased in a hard frown. It was bad for the police to be without a central control, but that was better than for control to be in the hands of the Blind Man. Jackson came back, saluted in the darkness.

"All set, major," he said crisply, using the title under which he and Wentworth had first met on the battlefields.

Wentworth nodded and strode to the car, climbed in front beside the wheel. Slowly, his jaw hardened. The Spider was going into battle. No man could say whether he would emerge from it with his life—but grimly the resolve had formed in Wentworth's brain: the Blind Man must be destroyed at all costs!

CHAPTER 9
THE BLIND MAN STRIKES

JUST BEFORE the car reached the fringe of the theatrical district, Wentworth entered the tonneau and set to work. It was a perilous thing he intended to do, but the Spider had never shrunk from that, if by risking his life he could better fight the enemy.

Ram Singh had transferred several packages from his own car

to that of the police. Wentworth opened these now, revealing a mirror attached to a flashlight which he propped on the coat rail before him, a make-up kit, a bundle of clothing.

From the make-up kit, he took a small vial. Pouring some of the liquid it contained on a small sponge, he smeared it on his face. The skin tautened over the bones, made the nose sharp and thin, the cheek bones more prominent. His complexion lost its healthy tan, became sallow and drawn. He painted out his lips so that his mouth became a straight gash; putty transformed his nose into a predatory beak and shadow sank his eyes into pits. That was all save for a wig of lank black hair, and shaggy brows to cover his own. Richard Wentworth was gone and in his place was—the Spider!

He shook out the clothing in the bundle, then draped a long black cape over his arm and pulled the wide brim of a black hat low over his eyes. A block from the theater which he had selected to cover, he alighted from the car, stopped for a moment to instruct Jackson.

"Leave the car, but don't follow me," he ordered. "If I want you, I'll summon you. Otherwise, keep out of the way of the bandits or you're apt to lose your eyes!"

Jackson alighted. "But, major, you mean I'm to just stand here no matter what…" He stopped then, seeing the tight smile on Wentworth's lips. "There are further orders, sir?" he asked diffidently.

Wentworth nodded. "There undoubtedly will be fugitives. When you are sure you have spotted a bandit, follow him. Finding his destination is a hundred times more important than any small good you could accomplish in the battle! The police are here to do the fighting. You know how to report."

Jackson saluted stiffly, "Yes, Major!"

With a nod, Wentworth was gone, striding briskly along toward the theater. His cane tapped rhythmically, his shoulders were thrown back. His face was the face of the Spider, but the Spider was best known by his cape and his carriage. Wentworth thought he would not have any difficulty in passing even the lines of suspicious police! But should any one of them recognize him... Wentworth's lips tightened. He would have to chance that!

Only a few late arrivals remained outside the theater beneath its brilliantly lighted marquee. The police were not in sight, but there were cars parked along the street where it was forbidden to park during this hour. Wentworth smiled slightly. The police had been prompt in taking their stations. He strolled into the outer lobby of the theater and purchased a standing room ticket. In that way, he would be less conspicuous and freer to move about. He cast a final glance about him and went inside.

The curtain had already risen, and the actors were romping through one of the hit farces of the year. Wentworth had small doubts that this would be one of the theaters raided. The Blind Man was after money and he would go where the prices were highest and popularity assured a big gate.

Swiftly, his eyes quested over the audience, the boxes, the stage. From what point would the Blind Man strike? The manager's office was on the second floor, across the lounge from the balcony and loge seats. That was where the receipts of the day would be counted as soon as the box office closed, but Wentworth was strangely reluctant to go there. A sixth sense seemed to warn him of danger lurking nearby—in his immediate vicinity. His muscles tensed, and his eyes probed the shadows.

Kirkpatrick's mere pressing of a bell button had brought the Blind Man's killers with ready, drawn guns. Did that not indicate foreknowledge of Wentworth's coming, of what he knew and planned? His suspicions of Linda returned. She might have been sincere in warning him of the theater raids, and yet have phoned to the Blind Man that he was visiting Kirkpatrick!

HE COULD not believe that he had eliminated all of the Blind Man's spies among the police in that brief battle in Kirkpatrick's office. Undoubtedly, the Blind Man was fore-

warned that there would be police guards at the theaters. In such wholesale orders as he had been compelled to give to get speedy action, there were certain to be leaks. Forewarned, what would the Blind Man do? Certainly not abandon his plans. To do so would be a confession of weakness to his men, and such leaders survived by strength alone. No, he would follow through with his raid, and he would arrange matters so that the police guard would be nullified....

Even as the solution came to Wentworth's mind he glimpsed movement in the orchestra. From among the musicians, through the small door by which they passed under the stage, a figure crept. Wentworth's hand flew to his automatic, then he paused. He might be wrong, of course. Did he dare risk killing an innocent man...? And yet, if this were his quarry, who could say if he would ever have another chance at him? But the possibility of sacrificing an innocent life made Wentworth hesitate, and in the meantime the movement ceased.

The musicians played through some rhythmic stuff and on the stage a girl and boy tapped out a counter rhythm with dancing feet. There was a chorus in cellophane. In the midst of that gaiety, a woman's scream burst out—shrill with hysterical terror, charged with fearful agony.

Only a moment did her cry ring out alone; then the three front rows of the audience struggled to their feet as one man with a hundred voices, all shouting, screaming in a bedlam of pain and terror.

On the stage, everything came to a dead standstill, then the girl dancer ran to the edge of the platform and tried to quell the incipient panic.

"Hey, hey!" she cried. "I'm the only one that's supposed to be dancing. Pipe down there! Don't crab my act!"

She was lovely and gallant there as she flung into a fury of frenzied dancing, but only for a moment. Then her hands flew to her eyes, and her cry rose above them all. She took a faltering step forward and pitched head first into the orchestra pit!

The girl ushers at the heads of the aisles near Wentworth turned to flee. Wentworth sprang to the nearest. "Go down the aisles to the left and open the exit doors!" he snapped. "You go down the right! Move, quickly! Or we'll all be blinded! We must have fresh air!"

A porter was brushing up cigarette butts from the carpet and Wentworth caught him by the arm. "Turn on the ventilating system full force!" he ordered. "Quickly!"

The man fled, his eyes all whites with terror. Wentworth sprang to the back row of seats, mounted to the rail that separated them from the main cross aisle at the rear.

"Stay where you are!" he shouted. "Cover your eyes with your palms, tightly! Stand still! The doors are being opened! In a few moments, the air will be clear again! Stand still! You'll be crushed if you stampede!"

A gun spoke from the orchestra pit and the bullet whipped past Wentworth's ear, plucked at his hat brim. Wentworth's gun roared an answer and a man leaped convulsively from the darkness and collapsed.

"Stand still!" Wentworth shouted to the audience. "The Spider orders it!"

The cape draped from his shoulders now and his back was no longer straight, but twisted in the hunched deformity that the world knew was the Spider! There was another shot from the pit. The man who fired was crouched where Wentworth could not hit him without danger of striking someone in the audience.

The screams still rang out. A man danced with the agony in his eyes, and scrambled up the aisle. A woman reeled out behind him, reaching after him with one hand as she flung the other to her eyes. And suddenly a whole block of men and women was scrambling after them. The woman stumbled and fell. The crowd pushed on, stepped on her, trampling her. Her screams died quickly. But now the exit doors had been thrown wide, and the roar of the ventilating system reached a crescendo.

Wentworth fired both his guns into the air, sent bullets screaming over the heads of the stampede. "Stop!" he shouted at them. "Halt—then walk slowly. I'll shoot the first person who runs!"

TERROR HALTED the foremost of the mob, but those behind pressed on. Others groveled in the aisles, plucking at their agony-seared eyes. Some lay motionless across the seats, tossed there by the panic, or overcome with pain.

"Here," Wentworth cried. "I'll set the time for your march. Sing… Sing…" He shouted out the words of the tune to which the chorus had been dancing and somewhere far back among the people, a woman's brave, clear voice took up the song. She covered both eyes with the palms of her hands, and her features were twisted with pain, but she sang. It was the dancing girl, that one who had fallen into the pit. She limped painfully. Her gay costume was torn, stained with blood from a wound in her shoulder, but she sang and others began to take up the air. The atmosphere of the theater was clearing, eddied by the open doors, the ventilating system.

Wentworth jumped from his perch, stepped from seat to seat as he pressed toward the orchestra pit. There was still a gunman there, lurking somewhere in the shadows, possibly spreading more of that devil's spray in the air.

As he advanced, he caught the glitter of moving metal. He bent sharply forward and fired as powder flame stabbed at him once more. A man screamed out hoarsely, voice muffled by the mask he wore. His cry was drowned in the singing, the garbled, half-hysterical chanting of the crowd as it streamed, orderly now, out of the building, through the lobby to the street.

There was no more the Spider could do here. He sprang to the aisle, helped to her feet a woman who had fallen there, then raced for the steps that led upward. The strategy of the Blind Man was simple and effective. Blind a few score people and stampede the audience. In the thick of the crowd, the bandits could escape with the loot. What did it matter if half a hundred people were maimed for life? What did it matter if the brave dancing girl would never prance across the boards again with her blithe song? A harsh sound forced itself out between Wentworth's locked teeth. By God, death was too good for the unfeeling monster who was called the Blind Man!

Up the crowded steps, Wentworth forced his way. Men and

women shrank from his path, and through the thick of the press ran the whisper, the cry: *"The Spider! The Spider!"* Wentworth smiled grimly. It was well. Let the whisper spread terror, then the men he sought would betray themselves. By heaven, he would let the Blind Man know he was fighting!

He whirled to his right toward the door of the manager's office, and a man standing there snatched out a gun. Wentworth laughed and squeezed the automatic in his hand. The man whipped forward, doubled at the belly as if he had received a terrific punch there. He had—the punch of the Spider's lead! His gun dropped from his hand and he whipped his arms across his stomach, kept his feet for a moment, then toppled forward on his face.

The man's shout had warned the others in the office. "Get back," Wentworth shouted at the crowd. "Get to cover. You're in no danger if you get to cover!"

He fired through the office door and inside a man yelped.

"Get to cover!" Wentworth cried again at the crowd.

From inside the office, a sub-machine gun stammered. Lead punched a ragged pattern in the door and Wentworth flung himself flat on the floor. Somewhere behind him, a boy's voice rose in shrill agony and then stopped. Wentworth rolled rapidly to his right, glanced behind him. Except for himself and that pitiful huddle that had been a living being a few moments before, the place was empty now. Wentworth sprang to his feet and reached the wall beside the door. He shouted, and the sound was fierce and menacing.

"The Spider comes for you!" he cried. "Prepare for death!"

The machine gun's stammer was almost hysterical. The middle of the door was eaten to ribbons. Through the hole the bullets had cut, Wentworth fired twice. He shot the lock off the door, kicked it open. He glimpsed the compensator of a submachine gun thrusting around the jamb toward him and slapped a forty-five calibre bullet against it. The machine gun whipped out of sight, a man cried out in numbed pain, and Wentworth stepped into clear sight, a gun in each hand.

THERE WERE three men on their feet. The machine gun lay on the floor and one of the men was diving to reach it. The other two threw up their revolvers, and Wentworth's two automatics spat together. There was no need for him to fire at those men a second time. The machine gunner snatched for his weapon, his hands still numb from the impact of the Spider's bullet.

"You can't use that gun again," Wentworth told him gently. "I smashed the compensator."

The man caught up the machine gun desperately, and Wentworth shot it from his hands a second time. He smashed the bullet against the weapon's trigger. The gun coughed once and the barrel flew apart. A fragment went through the gunner's chin, his face was split in half. He went backwards and did not stir again.

Wentworth cursed savagely. That was not what he wanted. Dead men couldn't talk. He whirled and strode from the office, and a policeman at the head of the steps flung up a gun. Wentworth darted aside, charged the man desperately. The first shot went wide, but the second could not miss at the shortened range. And Wentworth did not fire on the police! Despairingly, he hurled an automatic at the cop's face. The man dodged, his second bullet went wide, and he had no time for a third shot. The Spider's shoulder took him amidships and hurled him across the width of the hallway. Instantly, Wentworth was on his feet, had recovered his gun and the officer's and was leaping down the stairs. He whipped off the cape, thrust away his guns. A moment later he was pressing out of the theater in the tail of the departing audience.

A sergeant of police and a half dozen men were scanning faces anxiously as the crowd filed through. Two more police were worming their way inside. Wentworth went up to the sergeant.

"The Spider's fighting them up there!" he said excitedly. "Looked to me like the Spider got a bullet in the belly, and…" He had time to say no more. With a shout to his men, the sergeant waded through the crowd. There was no harm in removing the guard now, Wentworth thought with twisted lips. The criminals were dead. But that was less than justice. All about him were men and women who would never see again….

Abruptly, Wentworth whirled and hurried back into the theater, made his way toward the orchestra pit. There was a chance, just a chance that some of the Darkener remained in whatever container it had been carried in. If he could get a sample… With a muffled cry, he snatched up a small round tank with a hose connection, shook it and heard the slap of liquid within. He rushed out through the unguarded main entrance and hurried toward the place where Jackson waited.

"Not a crook came out that I could see," Jackson growled. "I heard shooting."

Wentworth nodded. "I killed them all." He handed the tank to Jackson. "Take this to Miss Nita. Don't let any of it escape, or it would blind you. I'll phone her instructions. And hurry, man."

"And you, Major?"

Wentworth smiled thinly. He had an automatic in his hand, stuffing a fully loaded clip into its butt. "I'm going to another theater, Jackson. It's just possible that the raid wasn't simultaneous everywhere, and… Get going, Jackson."

Jackson saluted and stalked away with the tank under his arm. For a moment longer, Wentworth delayed, then he strode off in the direction of the theater he had picked as the next most likely to be the scene of the Blind Man's activities. He paused for a moment to phone Nita.

"Dear, I'm sending you a tank by Jackson. It has some of the chemical that blinds people in it," he said rapidly. "Wear a mask that covers your eyes when you work on it, but see if you can analyze its contents. If we know what causes the blindness, it's possible we may be able to find an antidote."

Nita said quietly: "Yes, Dick. You're not coming home?"

"I'm going to try to find the Blind Man's headquarters!" Wentworth said harshly. "The fiend let loose the chemical on the entire audience of a theater." He paused to gain control of his voice. "Tell Kirkpatrick that, and ask him if, after that, he can still keep silent about what he knows of the Blind Man."

NITA'S VOICE was quiet but very somber. "Be brave, Dick," she whispered, "but be careful."

"Wait," Wentworth said sharply. "Something is wrong. I can tell by your voice... By God, *Kirkpatrick!* It must be. What is it?"

Nita drew in a slow breath. It made a hissing noise over the phone. "You'll have to know now, I suppose," she said. "Dick...."

"Yes, dear," Wentworth said sharply. "What is it? Did Kirkpatrick get away?"

"Yes, Dick, Kirkpatrick got away, and Linda ran away, and Ram Singh," Nita's voice broke... "Ram Singh is... *blind!*"

CHAPTER 10
THE SMOKE POTS

WENTWORTH WAS silent so long after Nita gave him her incredible news that she became anxious and called to him with sharp fear. Wentworth roused himself. Linda Carroll's disappearance confirmed her treachery. It was unimportant, but Ram Singh....

"Kirkpatrick... did that?" he asked.

"Ram Singh isn't sure. He had Kirkpatrick in the front seat beside him. He turned in that direction, and...."

Wentworth said heavily: "Do all you can for him, Nita. If you can analyze the fluid I'm sending you..." His voice harshened. "I'll be home soon. I'm hoping to take a prisoner in the meanwhile."

He swung from the phone booth and strode out, anger lengthening his stride. His pace bode ill to any minion of the Blind Man who crossed his path! He moved rapidly, eyes watchful for signs that the raiders were still at work. And such signs were plentiful. Men and women, who clasped hands to eyes in agony, ran wildly about the streets or crouched, groaning, against walls. On the curb a young man and a girl, lovely in gay dress, stood motionless, arms about each other. Their eyes stared sightlessly into space. Ambulances lined the street, and policemen strode energetically about, or stood grim guard over the injured. There was a strained, hopeless look on all their faces, for they had their casualties, too.

Wentworth left this first street of horror and sought other theaters where the attack might have been delayed. If he could get his hands on a prisoner, he would extort information from him. He would, by God, if he had to tear his victim slowly to bits! A fiend that would spread the blindness....

A third and a fourth theater Wentworth inspected, and all showed only emptiness. And, on the streets, in front of them were the pitiful victims. Some screamed and cursed; others were bravely silent—they were the more pitiable. Damn it, the robbery was complete, but surely the Blind Man could not yet have cleared all his forces from the scene. The bandits could not have fled from the doors of the theaters in cars, for police were on guard there; and to get past them, the men had necessarily fled on foot in the midst of the panic. They would have a rallying point where escape cars waited. Nothing so suspicious as cars parked on the street... Wentworth pivoted abruptly and stared along the dark way he had just come. A garage! That would be it, the cars parked and waiting in a garage....

With an oath, Wentworth threw himself into a hard sprint.

NITA VAN SLOAN

There was a garage half way up this block, and it was centrally situated. It would be easy for the bandits to meet there....

Openly, he strode into the building, but found no suspicious congregation of men. He flung into the office and demanded the telephone, called police headquarters and stated his suspicions in sharp sentences. Kirkpatrick was not there, but the official in charge pounced on the suggestion. Almost before Wentworth had left the garage, new sirens were whining nearby. In four or five minutes, every garage in the neighborhood, every parking lot would be covered by the police, men in gas masks whom the Darkener could not stop....

Wentworth got a taxi and started a swift round of the nearby garages himself. The police might come moments too late and the bandits escape....

A blast of guns came from a side street two blocks up Seventh Avenue. More than one submachine gun was chattering madly, and smaller arms made a wild tattoo.

"Hurry!" Wentworth urged the driver. "Fiftieth street...."

The taxi driver twisted about a pale face. "Not me, boss. Don't you hear them guns?"

Wentworth cursed and sprang to the pavement. "Get down," he snapped. "Here... Here's a hundred. You can say I stole the cab. Get down, damn you...."

The driver jumped from behind the wheel and Wentworth hurled the car swiftly forward, took the corner of Fiftieth on

squealing rubber. There were two police radio roadsters in the battle. One had been driven squarely across the gateway of a garage and wedged there. The driver was limp over the wheel, but the other man, crouched behind the engine of the car, was firing into the darkness of the building. The second roadster was parked at the curb, also blocking the driveway and the two men from it were pressed against the brick wall of the garage, firing around the jamb of the door.

AS WENTWORTH whirled to a stop, he saw a window on the second floor of the garage building shoot up, saw a sub-machine gun thrust out. It had blasted out a dozen bullets before Wentworth could fire. One of the policemen was hammered, clawing the wall, to the pavement. At the same instant, a heavy car charged out of the garage doorway. It picked up the light radio roadster of the police, turned it over on top of the man who crouched behind. He screamed once, twice, then the sliding roadster ground over his chest and he was silent. The third policeman, alone alive, sprang to the running board of the fleeing car and fired point blank into the driver's skull.

The driver's head was blown half off, but a moment later a machine gun's gale of lead struck the policeman. He was blown to the pavement—and even then the rain of leaden death did not stop. He was pinned against the curb, riddled. Another of the occupants of the car had seized the wheel, was trying to steer while still another opened the door to thrust out the dead driver.

Wentworth darted forward and seized the machine gun of the man he had slain in the second story window. The gun had dropped, cushioned by the body of the dead policeman. In

Wentworth's hands, the tommy gun became an avenging demon. A single short burst smashed the two bandits who were trying to handle the reeling car, and it bumped the curb, ground its nose into the brick side of a theater building and remained there. A gun spoke once from its tonneau, the machine gun chattered again and all was still.

Wentworth flung himself to the pavement in the shelter of the overturned police ear, crouched there with the ready sub-machine gun. He could not see into the garage entrance, but anyone who attempted to crash out there would face certain death at his hands. More police sirens were screaming toward him now. In a few moments, the gang would be bottled up…

Through the garage door hurtled a small black object. It hit the bottom of the overturned car, bounded back. Wentworth gasped, crouched behind the engine and the bomb let go. The car leaped, fragments of the grenade bored through its tinny sides, banged against the engine. The concussion almost stunned Wentworth, but an instant after it let go, he reared up with the machine gun ready. He was just in time. Through the broad doorway hurtled a car already doing thirty miles an hour and accelerating every moment. Its front bumper ticked the rear of the overturned car, hurled it toward Wentworth.

With a shout of hard laughter, Wentworth leaped aside and squeezed the trigger of the machine gun. A man screamed and the car, in the middle of a skidding turn, straightened out wildly, skidded broadside and—rolled. But the second machine already was thunderbolting from the garage. A half dozen guns blazed inside the garage. Wentworth hit the pavement fast. His protecting shield, the overturned car, had been kicked out of the way by the repeated impacts of the fleeing machines, and this sedan… He saw that the men fired through narrow ports in the glass, and recognized at once that this fugitive car was bulletproofed.

Quick as thought, he jerked down the muzzle of the machine gun and held steadily on the left front wheel. The spokes were wood and the bullets of the machine gun were forty-five cali-bre. He had only two seconds, but the gun in that time could fire ten bullets. For moments, he thought that he had failed. The car raced with gathering speed along the street. From its rear, Wentworth saw bombs tossed. But these instead of exploding with a terrific detonation made cracks like pistol shots and sent towers of black, roiling vapor a dozen feet in the air. The towers subsided *slowly*, spreading, filling the street from wall to wall. Behind it, Wentworth heard the ripping crash of a collision and a cold smile parted his lips. He had not, after all, failed. But that black vapor which was taking on a yellowish cast now, what was it? He thought he knew all right. That would be the Darkener, the vapor that blinded….

While his eyes kept keen watch, he fumbled with the dead policeman beside him, stripping the gas mask from his head. A grenade from within the garage missed him only because it rolled into the gutter and the solid concrete screened Went-worth from it.

Wentworth lay motionless, his senses reeling, the gas mask free in his hand. Slowly, he forced the hand toward his face. That pain in his side… He was lying on the machine gun. His eyes

were dull, half blinded. God, that man in the window with a gun.
He couldn't miss a motionless, helpless target....

WENTWORTH GATHERED all his strength and rolled
half over. A bullet splashed on the pavement almost against his
face, and the particles of hot lead stung. Two cars thunderbolted
out of the garage and another bomb exploded farther away.
Black, roiling gas spewed upward, crawled along the ground.
The man up there in the window was taking very careful aim
this time. Wentworth had an automatic in his fist now, but to
raise it seemed an impossible task... He couldn't....

The blast of his own gun startled him. His hand was so numb
he had scarcely realized it was pointed.

The man in the window flinched as brick dust sprayed into
his face. His bullet went wide and Wentworth fired again, a
third time. It was the last bullet that did it. Hit under the breast
bone, the killer in the window threw back his head and opened
his mouth to shout. No sound came out, he pitched forward
over the sill, lay that way for seconds before he slumped out into
space. His head broke open on the pavement.

Full consciousness returned to Wentworth again. The
sub-machine gun was in his hands. There was a stinging in his
eyes, and he realized that already the greasy black vapor, that
carried a strange tinge of yellow, was crawling about his feet.
With an oath, he drew the gas mask over his head. A final car
whipped out of the garage, Wentworth threw up the machine
gun... only three shots spat from its muzzle, and already the
car had vanished into the smoke screen that the Darkener had
made.

Wentworth dropped the chopper and made his way heavily along the street. He paused for a moment to press his Spider's seal to the cheek of the man he had shot from the window. The Blind Man would hear and know that it was the Spider who had wrought such fearful carnage among his men this day. Three car loads of his killers stopped in mid-flight. He did not know how many had been killed, but all of the wrecks had been complete except the first, and in that car, four men had been killed by gun fire… He pushed on through the black vapor. It was risky. He did not know how effective the gas mask would be against the Darkener, and in the murk he might easily be mistaken by police for one of the bandits. But he had a task to do. If any of the Blind Man's creatures remained alive….

In the first car, there were only corpses. The second contained two dead, and the rest of its occupants had fled. He went heavily on toward the third car, but at a distance, saw a policeman standing beside the wreck. For a moment, he debated overpowering the officer—but decided it would be futile. Any live bandits must already have been removed. Wentworth faded away into the darkness.

His movements were heavy with fatigue. The concussion of those blasts had taken their toll, though he had escaped direct injury. For the men killed, he felt no regret. What they meted out at the orders of the Blind Man was many times worse than death. He remembered that girl and boy with their arms about each other, blind for the rest of their lives. Brave Ram Singh… The Spider's fist clenched. Where, in the name of God, would all this end?

CHAPTER 11
NEW TREACHERY

DESPITE HIS fatigue, Wentworth hastened to his home. Jenkyns opened service door to him and insisted that he have a rub-down at once. Jenkyns' face wore a solicitous expression, but worry lurked in his eyes—worry that would never be erased, Wentworth knew, until Sue and Hal Moran were out of the danger that beset them all.

Wentworth laughed softly, clapped Jenkyns on the shoulder. "All right, as soon as I've spoken to Miss Nita."

"In the laboratory, sir," Jenkyns reported and Wentworth strode through the long living room into the high-ceilinged music conservatory. One entire end was taken up by an organ, and Wentworth moved directly to it, raised his hands and patted the orifices of some of the smaller pipes. The air columns vibrated and the ghost of a tune wailed in the tubes. He left them and strode along the paneled wall, paused before one section. It receded, then slid noiselessly aside and Wentworth stepped through and closed it behind him.

Nita had heard the operation of the mechanism and came across the small hidden room in which Wentworth kept his disguises; where, also, he had installed a small, efficient laboratory. They spoke no word of greeting, but Nita crept into his arms and pressed her head against his chest. Wentworth's arms closed tightly about her. How near, how near he had been this night to death... He laughed softly. "How goes the experiment, Nita?"

97

Nita looked up into his face, touched with her fingertips the small wounds that splintered bullet fragments had made. She drew his lips down to hers... Presently, she was again the brisk assistant Wentworth knew.

"Ram Singh remained entirely blind for about an hour," she said, her voice wooden with its suppression of grief over the valiant Sikh. "Then he recovered his sight partially. That has been the situation for a little more than three hours now, but it seems to me that his vision is failing gradually again. In approximately five hours after the liquid struck his eyes, I think he will be totally blind again."

Wentworth closed his jaw tightly. "And the Darkener? Have you finished an analysis?"

Nita led him to the laboratory bench, pointed to a notebook in which her crisp, even handwriting had made a long table of symbols. Wentworth bent over it, exclaimed sharply.

"That's approximately the composition of the venom of the cobra *rhingals*," he cried.*

---

* AUTHOR's NOTE: The South African cobra, *rhingals*, or *sepedon hamachates*, is unique among poisonous reptiles in that it makes no attempt to bite its victims, but sprays venom at its victim's eyes. This is done by closing the mouth sharply as if biting, thus exerting pressure on the venom glands and ejecting the venom in a fine spray from the duct orifices in the fangs, very much on the principle of a hypodermic syringe. The cobra rhingals, indigenous to Africa, is phenomenally accurate at distances of six to eight feet. Its venom causes excruciating pain in the eyeballs, blindness, and, in the course of five to six hours, death in convulsions. Wentworth deduced from

"Arsenic in it, too," Nita said quietly. "I think we may expect death in some cases. Depending, of course, on how much of the active substance reached the eyes. I put compresses of hydrated sesquioxide of iron* on Ram Singh's eyes and afterward washed

the analysis Nita had made of the Darkener that the Blind Man had created a synthetic substitute which retained the blinding qualities of the venom without the death-dealing properties. As a general rule, if the chemical properties of a poison are known, it is possible to counteract it chemically by administering an antidote which will unite with the poison to form a non-harmful compound. Wentworth's problem in this case was to find such a compound and antidote which would not harm the eyes. It goes without saying that the antidote must be administered before the poison has had an opportunity to set up physiological complications. Such complications, of course, would have to be treated separately from a medicinal standpoint. I am unable to account for the brief recurrence of vision after the initial hour of blindness, unless this original blindness was not actual, but caused by the shock and pain of the Darkener striking the eyeball.

* AUTHOR'S NOTE: Hydrated sesquioxide of iron is the chemical antidote for arsenic in its usual form of arsenious acid, which is the oxide of arsenic. Nita, in applying the antidote to Ram Singh's eyes, showed rare good judgment. For arsenic is readily absorbed into the system through any membrane, and has been known to kill when applied to an open sore. The antidote unites with the arsenious acid to form a non-soluble arsenite of iron. Because this form of arsenic is not soluble in body fluids, it, of course, cannot cause any further harm. Arsenic poison, even when administered *per ora* often affects the sight, making the eyes sensitive to light, and at some stages of poisoning, blinding the victim almost completely.

99

them with boracic acid. There was quite a quantity of the arsenite of iron."

"Good girl!" Wentworth cried. "That undoubtedly saved Ram Singh's life! Damn the men who did this! If it was Kirkpatrick...." He fell silent, but his face darkened with angry blood. PRESENTLY, HE threw off the anger that shook him and told Nita briefly what he thought would serve as an antidote for the Darkener.

"It will be highly volatile," he said slowly, "and the distilling process will have to be performed at low temperature to prevent carrying over into the condenser other harmful chemicals. If you'll start that, I'll go have a look at Ram Singh and clean myself up a bit." His hand went to his wounded cheek, and his lips twisted wryly. He had paid back that score many-fold.

Ram Singh squatted against the wall in his room, his turbaned head erect, his blind eyes staring straight ahead of him. His head swung toward Wentworth and, after a moment, he rose to his feet and salaamed.

"*Sahib!*" he muttered.

Wentworth crossed and put a hand on his shoulder, clamped down hard with his fingers. "There will be a vengeance for this, warrior!" he said thickly. "Can you see at all, Ram Singh?"

The Sikh shook his head, a ghost of a smile touched his bearded lips. "*Sahib*, thy servant recognized thee by thy step, which is light and fierce as the *bagh*, the tiger. And, *sahib*, thou need not worry about thy servant's vengeance." His hand went to the knife at his side. "In the Punjab hills, we have fought at night, *sahib*. Cast some object against the wall."

Wentworth gazed thoughtfully at the Sikh, feeling his throat tighten. Ram Singh was meeting his affliction with character-istic courage. Wentworth picked up a cushion from the floor, tossed it lightly against the wall. There was a glitter of steel as Ram Singh's knife swished through the air. It caught the pillow and pinned it to the wall almost at the point it had struck, so swift had been the Sikh's throw. Ram Singh stood with arms folded across his deep chest, turbaned head held high.

"*Sahib,* thy servant will perform his own vengeance!"

Wentworth gripped his shoulder once more and left without speaking. He was silent, too, under Jenkyns' ministrations but slowly, beneath prodding fingers, his fine-toned muscles began to respond. An alcohol rubdown completed his revivification and he went to the laboratory with his great vigor fully restored. For two hours, Nita and Wentworth worked side by side in the laboratory. Finally, they were ready to begin the process of distil-lation, and Wentworth and Nita lifted weary heads.

"Better get some sleep, dear," Wentworth told her. "It will be close to four hours before this run is finished. When that's done…."

Nita came to him slowly. "But Ram Singh…."

Wentworth's lips tightened. He shook his head slowly. "The Darkener has finished its work on him. Doctors may be able to help. We can't."

"You don't think doctors can help either, Dick?"

"I'm afraid not, dear. Get some sleep now."

They moved together toward the door of the hidden room and Wentworth stopped in his tracks, listening tensely. He had a listening post in this nearly sound-proof room, a microphone pickup system… He reached the loudspeaker attachment in a long stride and adjusted the volume. Jenkyns' voice came quaveringly….

"But I don't understand, Mr. Kirkpatrick," he said. "You have a warrant for… Master Dick?"

Kirkpatrick's crisp, metallic voice overrode his. "Search the place, sergeant. Bring every person in it to me here."

Wentworth whispered, "Ram Singh! He'll kill Kirkpatrick! I'll have to go out there!"

Nita's hand closed on his arm. "No, Dick! He has a warrant for you! If you're arrested, you can't… can't fight the Blind Man. You can't do anything. They won't let Ram Singh hurt Kirkpatrick."

IN THE dim light of the small room, Wentworth faced Nita. He caught her shoulders and gazed deeply into her eyes.

"I've got to take a gamble," he said swiftly, "and it doesn't appear to me to be much of a risk. I don't think Kirkpatrick will take me to jail. He will turn me over to the Blind Man and report that I escaped!"

"But, Dick…."

"Dear, I haven't much time. Jackson is to follow and report back to you. If I'm taken to jail, get a writ of habeas corpus through my lawyer. But I won't be. Darling, I have to do it! I haven't a tangible clue in the world to the Blind Man. By letting him take me prisoner… He won't want to kill me right away. I've balked him too many times. He'll prefer to torture me. That will give Jackson time to get you and Ram Singh…."

"Ram Singh! But he's blind, Dick. And Jackson and I aren't strong enough…."

Wentworth told her rapidly of Ram Singh's skill in his darkness. "Please, dear, no more now. I've got to hurry." He crossed the room to the second entrance, which gave on the service steps outside his apartment. He glanced out through the peep-hole to see that everything was clear.

Nita's arms closed about him. "Oh, Dick, Dick… I feel— Dick, I'm not superstitious. You know that. But I feel that something terrible impends. It's wrong, Dick. You mustn't put yourself in his power! If you do—if you do…."

Wentworth felt cold touch his heart for a moment. Nita was not superstitious, God knew, nor was he. But Nita did not fear foolishly. More than once before she had known these premonitions of disaster, and never had she been wrong. His lips shut grimly. It couldn't be helped. There was no other way.

He crushed her close in his arms, their lips clung… He tore himself away, twisted the lever that operated the door and stepped out into the hall. He had a hat, cane and gloves snatched from his disguise rack.

"Au 'voir m'amie!" he called, and closed the door of the secret room—closed it on Nita's sob, and strode, frowning, toward the front door of his apartment. Her apprehensions sat heavily upon him. With a shrug he threw off the depression, unlocked the door and stopped in assumed amazement as he saw two policemen just inside. Kirkpatrick, hands clasped behind him, stood in the middle of the drawing room. Wentworth nodded to the officers and went past them.

"Hello, Kirk," he said quietly. "Were you looking for me?"

Kirkpatrick nodded, the saturnine lines of his face unchanged. "I have a warrant for your arrest, Wentworth," he said coldly. "Murder in the first degree. You've overstepped yourself this time, killing policemen in the very office of the commissioner!"

Wentworth stared at him in amazement for a moment. He started to laugh, but the seriousness of Kirkpatrick's face stopped that. He took a step forward, "Surely, you can't be serious, Kirk!" he said. "You know as well as I do that they weren't policemen, that they were the agents of the Blind Man attempting to kill me. Why, you even killed one yourself, shot him down when he was holding a gun on me!"

Kirkpatrick's lips twisted in a taut smile. He lifted a hand and parted his black, military mustaches with thumb and forefinger. "Sorry, Wentworth, it won't work. You tried to keep me from putting a guard around the theaters. When I summoned men to help me, you killed them, took me prisoner, but not until I had succeeded in giving the orders to guard."

Wentworth set his fists on his hips. "Kirkpatrick," he said coldly, "you're the damnedest liar that ever lived! You're in league with the Blind Man, and a cold-blooded crook. You blinded Ram Singh…."

Wentworth's anger foamed to his brain. For a moment, he was on the point of hurling himself at Kirkpatrick, but the Commissioner only smiled at him faintly, and looking behind him, Wentworth saw that two policemen held guns *leveled* at his back. They hadn't challenged. They were waiting for Wentworth to attack, so they could kill.

Wentworth threw back his head and laughed, and the mockery of it was bitter in his throat.

"No, no, better not shoot, Kirkpatrick," he cried. "Your master, the Blind Man, would prefer to have me alive for a while." He stopped laughing and smiled coldly into Kirkpatrick's face. "You treacherous dog!" he said clearly.

The blow came from behind without any warning. Cold white light exploded in his brain and Wentworth pitched limply forward on his face.

CHAPTER 12
IN THE ENEMY'S POWER

WENTWORTH HAD to fight his way back to consciousness. His fatigue, the exhaustion of long hours of futile struggle, worked against him. When finally his senses were fully returned, he realized that he was slumped down in the rear seat of a car between two men. The car whirred swiftly along through the brightly sunlit streets of New York. This he saw through half-opened eyes which ached with the repercussions of the blow which Kirkpatrick's man had dealt him. He saw also that he was not in the section of the city between his own home and police headquarters, as he would be if this were a normal arrest. He laughed softly.

The men beside him jerked about, guns leveled in their fists, and Wentworth opened his eyes their full width, smiled slowly upon them. His captors did not wear police uniforms. One glance at their faces confirmed his earlier guess. Kirkpatrick had turned him over to the minions of the Blind Man.

His smile twisted into bitterness. It was inconceivable, even when he knew it for fact, that the man who had been his friend through these many years of conflict with the Underworld, should turn him over to his enemies. He brushed aside the gloomy mood. He had read the signs aright. By this time, Jackson was on his trail and, when they had reached their destination, would summon Nita and Ram Singh to help him destroy this emperor of darkness!

Wentworth had no illusions concerning the size of the task ahead. He knew that, even if Jackson succeeded in shadowing the car without being detected, it would be a task of staggering proportions for those three to smash their way into the Blind Man's stronghold. Wentworth must meantime gain his freedom so as to assist them. Their goal was not merely rescue. Wentworth had subjected himself to this peril for the sole purpose of finding the Blind Man. When he was free, he must destroy his captor!

Wentworth shrugged aside such thoughts and inspected his immediate surroundings. His hands were shackled and fastened to the coat rack on the back of the front seat, so that his body was strained forward uncomfortably, supported by the handcuffs. In addition, the guns of his captors were held unwaveringly upon him.

He glanced curiously at the streets through which they passed, and noted that his guards were unconcerned that he did so. That fact was ominous. It meant plainly that the Blind Man never would let him have an opportunity to follow that route.

"Careless of you," Wentworth reproved the man on his right. "I can see very plainly that we're going up the Grand Concourse. When I get free I can lead the raiders right to you."

Without a word, the man on his right reached out and dragged the muzzle of his gun down across Wentworth's cheek and mouth. It was cruelly done, and the slow drip of blood followed in the path of the pain.

Wentworth's lips curved stiffly in a smile. He looked into the eyes of the man who had hurt him, and the man quailed. His prisoner was bound helpless and he himself held a gun in his hand, yet the man cowered under the flick of the Spider's gaze. Afterward he blustered, but Wentworth had seen and understood. When the time came, he would use his knowledge of the man's fear to good purpose.

Wentworth remained silent then throughout the rest of the trip and the men with him on the rear seat and the driver, were silent, too. The car bored steadily into the prim suburbs of Westchester, and turned finally from the main road to climb steadily up a private driveway that wound through a thick grove of trees.

After a short climb, the car stopped before a towering gate of solid steel set in a high stone wall. When the car and its occupants had been fully inspected by a guard, the gates swung open and the machine crawled through. Another half mile of up grade and they came to a stop before a rambling stone house which crowned the hill.

Wentworth frowned at sight of the building. He knew it

perfectly, had visited here several times. It belonged to the broker-financier at whom many of the Blind Man's attacks had been leveled—Walter Smythe! At one time, Wentworth had entertained some thought that the man might himself be the Blind Man, but all suspicions had necessarily died when the man's own daughter had been blinded. Smythe's grief had been genuine. Yet here was the Blind Man, holding forth in the Smythe's summer residence!

FOUR MORE men with drawn revolvers came to the sides of the car before Wentworth's wrists were freed from the coat rail. They managed this by placing a second pair of handcuffs on his wrists outside the railing before the pair that secured him to the car was released. Then, surrounded by the four new guards, and the two who had brought him captive to the place, Wentworth was ushered up the broad steps, through the main entrance and into the drawing room of the house. There, comfortably ensconced in a large chair, was the Blind Man!

Through long moments, neither Wentworth nor the leader of the criminal band spoke. The Blind Man's characterization was perfect. He was a burlesque of the street mendicant. His suit was frayed and worn, a drab unpressed and uncleaned brown. In the house, he still wore his battered old hat and carried the cane with which he would *tap-tap* his way along the sidewalks. Large, dark glasses covered his eyes and into the band of his hat, he had tucked a sign which read:

I Am Blind!
Please help me

The man was a mockery and a jibe at every blind creature in the world, a taunt to the hundreds who were blind because of his thieving machinations and the dread chemical which he had loosed upon an innocent public. Wentworth's shoulders swelled. He felt wrath, hot and burning, rise in his chest—and hands clapped abruptly on his shoulders and yanked him backward. Guns ground into his ribs. The Blind Man got slowly to his feet, the cane stretching out before him. There was a guard beside his chair, and the guard shrank back, cowering at the mere lift of that cane.

Wentworth remembered the previous threat of that deadly implement, a touch of which might blind, or paralyze, or terribly kill…. He forced himself to calmness. He was not yet ready to force battle. Life and triumph must be won through delay while Jackson rushed off for reinforcements… He wondered how long he had been unconscious and how Kirkpatrick had transferred his prisoner to the crooks….

"I have you to thank," the Blind Man's voice held the monotonous, withdrawn tone of the afflicted, "for a partial failure last night, it seems."

Wentworth bowed suavely, hindered a little by the hands on his shoulders. "I am glad to hear it," he said pleasantly. "I am sorry the failure was only partial."

The Blind Man's dark glasses held steadily on his face, a slight smile twitched at the Blind Man's lips. "Later, you will not be sorry," he said. "I make it a principle to punish only in proportion to offense. If this had been a total failure…" He shrugged a little and his cane groped over the floor. Men moved from its path. The Blind Man raised his voice a little. *"Sue!"* he called.

From the dim reaches of the room, a girl came rapidly forward, and Wentworth's eyes went to her face, remembering Hal Moran, remembering old Jenkyns, who was this girl's uncle. This was Sue Moran, whom he had sworn to help.

Wentworth's smile of greeting was grim. Jenkyns' plea had been not for justice, but for mercy. If this girl received her just desserts… Wentworth studied her face. There was nothing cruel about its lines, only self-indulgence and vanity. She was a pretty thing, dark-haired, blue-eyed, with a mouth and a smile to drive men mad. Lovely blue eyes—but they reminded Wentworth of other eyes, of the blue, smiling eyes of Smythe's golden daughter that were blue no more—that were blind!

Wentworth bowed to her sardonically. "I see you still have your eyes. But you won't for long. Have they blinded your brother yet?"

Almost at the Blind Man's side, Sue jerked to a halt, then strode toward Wentworth lithely, her eyes stretching with anger. She stared at him, then whirled to the Blind Man.

"Who is this?" she demanded, her voice harsh. "Who is this—and why do you let him say things like that to me?"

"This is Mr. Wentworth," said the Blind Man, smiling, "who, the commissioner says, is the Spider. Whether he is the Spider or not, he has done enough to interfere with our plans. We have decided to… repay him."

SUE MORAN looked back at Wentworth and some of the

hatred left her eyes. In its place, there was dread, a touch of fright.

"Have you seen any of those victims of the Darkener?" Wentworth asked her softly. "You know, your brother's sweetheart was blinded that way. All the color is gone from her eyes, and she can't see anything at all. Now you…."

A shudder trembled over Sue Moran's fine body. She turned away from Wentworth and covered her face with her hands.

"Why do you let him say things like that to me?" she whimpered.

The Blind Man moved his cane in a gesture and the hands on Wentworth's shoulder hauled him backward and away.

"Your eyes will be like that some day!" Wentworth called to her. "When he is finished with you, you will be blinded, too!"

A gun struck painfully across the back of his skull, and one of his captors growled a warning. The Blind Man, Wentworth saw through aching eyes, had taken Sue Moran into his arms, had lowered his lips to her shining hair….

In the hall outside the door of the drawing room, his captors halted and pinned Wentworth against the wall, waiting.

One man muttered to another, "I thought the chief meant to put him away."

Another shook his head. "Not until he's shown him his picture gallery!" The men's chuckles rumbled together.

The wait in the hallway was prolonged, but presently the Blind Man came, alone now, his cane tapping a way ahead of him across the drawing room. He stopped just inside the door, pointing with his stick. The hands closed on Wentworth's shoulders again, thrust him along the hall. They went down cellar stairs and stopped before a doorway. One of the men swung the door wide, and Wentworth cursed sharply. He was gazing through steel bars into a cell, and against the wall three persons were chained, Hal Moran, Jimmy Carroll and—his sister, Linda! Wentworth had forgotten her. How had she left his house? Her blind face swung toward him dumbly, then he was snatched back, and the outer door of the cell clapped shut.

The room was dark when the second door was opened. A grating clanged aside and Wentworth was thrust through. Gyves were fastened to ankles, wrists and throat, holding him upright against the wall, and then the men clumped back across the room, but Wentworth was conscious of a presence before him. It was the voice of the Blind Man which spoke….

"I grant you the boon of light," he said softly. "You will want to use your eyes… while you have them."

Then he, too, stumped across the room behind the tapping of his cane, the steel grating clanged shut, the outer door thudded.

For a moment, there was the utter black darkness of a pit, then lights dazzled Wentworth's eyes, burning down blindingly from the ceiling. It was seconds before he could see, then a great cry rose in his throat, a cry of despair and anger and utter defeat. For there were three other persons chained to the walls of the room, three persons on whom all life, all hope depended… Jackson, Ram Singh and his beloved, Nita van Sloan!

CHAPTER 13
PREY OF THE DARKENER!

FOR MOMENTS, Wentworth's despair was too deep for words. He stared at the three who were fellow prisoners, but mostly his eyes sought those of Nita. She had warned him against submitting to capture, had told him of cold presentiments of disaster—and he had persisted. Disaster had claimed him, but there was no reproach in Nita's brave smile, no mention of her forebodings fulfilled. Her eyes told him of her love, her smile encouraged him….

"Not exactly what we'd planned, is it, dear?" she said quietly.

Jackson wrenched at his chains. His broad-jawed face was red with anger. The knotted muscles bulged in his cheeks.

"It's all my fault, Major!" he growled. "I let them see me following, and…."

Ram Singh did not speak. His blind eyes stared straight before him, unwinking, hopeless, but there was grimness about his bearded lips.

Nita interrupted Jackson. "I've told him, Dick, several times. It wasn't his fault. The police had scarcely left when the Blind Man's gang came for us. It was these men who saw Jackson and took him prisoner. They ran his car into a ditch, took him while he was stunned from the accident."

Wentworth forced a smile to his lips. He shook his head. "Everything is not lost. I have already set a plan to work here against the Blind Man. And Jenkyns is free. He will guess what is wrong, even if... Why, what's the matter? Was Jenkyns... hurt?"

Jackson stared at him wordlessly, then dropped his eyes. Nita bit her lips, her brave smile faltering.

"Jenkyns!" Wentworth cried. "Is he... dead?"

Nita shook her head slowly. "Jenkyns... betrayed us, Dick. He let the enemy in by the service entrance!"

Wentworth's arms strained against the shackles. "Jenkyns! Betrayed you! No, no. It isn't possible. You're mistaken. Surely, he..." Nita's eyes pitied him, but there was no wavering in the certainty of her expression. "Tell me," Wentworth said grimly.

Nita shrugged. "There isn't a great deal to tell. I don't think he intended to turn me over to them, but I had just left the laboratory, and was with Jackson, when Jenkyns led the men in. He seemed surprised to find me..." She laughed. "There can't be any doubt, Dick. He came here with us and was received and complimented by the Blind Man. Jenkyns is to receive ten thousand dollars and Hal Moran's life in return."

A slow frown gathered between Wentworth's eyes. That was the way the Blind Man worked, of course, forcing unwilling service by holding loved ones captive, compelling Linda to spy on him by threatening Hal, doing the same thing to Hal; and now Jenkyns had been bought into treachery by threats against his nephew. The money certainly would not have tempted him. Wentworth had settled ample funds upon Jenkyns... But to have surrendered Nita into the enemy's hands! Nita, whom Jenkyns loved even more devotedly than his master, than his own life... Wentworth shook his head heavily.

"You have some plan?" Nita suggested quietly, and Wentworth knew she sought to take his mind from his troubles as much as any other thing.

Wentworth smiled at her. It seemed a little foolish even to talk of plans, when they all were fastened upright against the walls, bound by steel at wrist, ankle and throat.

"We'll wait and see if it begins to work," he told them, "before I call it a plan." He looked about the room. The ceiling was raftered, unfinished, the walls about them were cement, and there was no opening in the room save the door by which they had entered, closed by steel grating and heavy wooden door.

In the silence that fell among them, Ram Singh spoke, "I have now two wrongs to avenge, then I shall be content to die! A man I have called comrade has been untrue to his salt!"

"Wait before you pass judgment, warrior," Wentworth said softly. "Jenkyns, by his treachery, has gained friendly entry to the enemy's stronghold!"

Nita gazed at him, but only pity remained in her eyes. Those of Jackson kindled slowly. He laughed boomingly.

"By the gods!" he whispered. "By the gods! Did you plan this, Major?"

WENTWORTH SAID nothing. There was no use undeceiving Jackson, if his hopes pointed that way. Jenkyns' betrayal was a cruel blow to them all. He smiled and while he encouraged them, the lights blinked out. It was as if the Blind Man knew that he had inflicted what torture he could with light, and gave them now the uncertainty of darkness lest they encourage each other. For a while after darkness fell, they all were silent, then

Wentworth called to ask Nita if she had had a chance to test the antidote for the Darkener which he had devised.

"No," Nita said quietly. "I have about two cubic centimeters of the antidote in a test-tube with me. I had it in my hand when we were captured and secreted it, but I had no chance to test it. I started a new and larger run just before I left the laboratory."

"You mean you left it in operation?" Wentworth asked quickly.

Nita's assent was quiet. "I tried a few drops of the fluid on my own eyes and it is painless, but whether it will help, I don't know, of course."

Wentworth started to answer her when a sound caught his ear, and he turned his head, tensely listening. The sound came again, and apprehension dragged coldly through his veins. He could not be mistaken. That had been the hiss of a snake.

He began talking, swiftly, without object, to drown it out. No need for the others to hear. This was more of the Blind Man's torture, whether the snake were loose or a prisoner, torture of the mind, the fear of things crawling in the dark… If he could keep the others from hearing, there would be no torture save for him.

Without other warning than the hiss, a fine spray struck Wentworth's face. He just suppressed a cry. Good God, could it be a cobra of the variety that sprayed its venom! But it had missed his eyes. It had missed… He turned his head aside, closed his eyes tightly and talked on and on, telling Nita that there was hope, reassuring Jackson and Ram Singh that his plan would work, that Jenkyns had come to help rather than betray.

If his friends detected the falsity of his accents, they made no comment. The spray hit again, struck the side of his throat!

And now the hiss was so near that Nita, nearest to him, heard the sound and cried out. "Dick, a snake! I heard a snake hiss!"

Wentworth laughed. "Nonsense!" he said, but his voice wavered. It was not for himself he feared, but if the snake attacked Nita. "Close your eyes!" he ordered sharply. "A cobra...."

Something glided over Wentworth's foot, rested there heavily. He could not even move his other foot to crush it, gyved as he was to the wall. And Nita... Wentworth clamped his jaw shut. The cobra's venom would be a too easy death for him. The Blind Man would not will him to die so easily, and in the darkness, there would be no way of telling which of the prisoners the cobra might strike. He laughed abruptly.

"Sorry, dear," he said. "I shouldn't have been taken in by such a trick. If there is a snake in the room, it is harmless. The Blind Man only seeks to torture us."

Nita said, "Of course. I should have guessed that."

The lights flared abruptly, and Wentworth glanced down at the floor, stood staring rigidly. He could not mistake the markings of the black and gray-banded snake that lay across his foot. It was a rhingals, one of the African cobras which sprayed its venom! Yet he could not be mistaken in his judgment. The Blind Man would not so risk his death. The answer obviously was that the snake had been rendered harmless.

Wentworth stirred his foot and the snake writhed upward, coiling, expanding its great hood and swaying. It struck at him— and nothing happened! Wentworth laughed.

"Now try something else, Blind Man!" he called. It was clear that they were being constantly watched and the knowledge made his heart sink. He was banking his hopes on Sue Moran rather than Jenkyns, though it was inconceivable that the aged butler could have betrayed him and suffered no pangs of conscience. Either way, it could not help if he were under watch at all times....

The outer door opened abruptly, and in the opening was framed the lovely figure of... *Sue Moran!*

THE GIRL spoke disdainfully to a man who appeared beside her. "Did you think that worn-out trick would fool him?" she demanded. "Take the snake out of there, and quit bothering the prisoners or the chief shall know of it!"

The man sneered. "Hell, he'd like it!"

Sue turned wholly toward the man. "You are probably right," she said sweetly. "He only spent twenty thousand dollars to capture this man, and I'm sure that he won't care to see him tortured himself. Just bought him as a plaything for the boys."

The man shrank back. "Don't tell on me, Miss Moran!" he pleaded. "Please don't tell on me! I didn't know! And I ain't hurt them. I just put the snake in there and used some water in that spray gadget that lets down out of the ceiling!"

"Take the snake out," Sue ordered again, more imperiously. And when the man had caught the reptile, she ordered him to leave and close the doors. "The chief wants me to ask them some questions."

"You sure you're safe in here with them, Miss Moran?" the man asked fawningly.

Sue smiled slightly, looked at the prisoners and their shackles. "Yes, I'm sure," she said. The man backed out and closed both doors. Sue Moran came rapidly forward, stood before Wentworth. There was belligerence in her manner, defiance, yet a certain fear. "What did you mean upstairs about him blinding me?" she demanded.

Wentworth smiled at her, but shook his head. The girl stepped closer. "Please, you've got to tell me." She glanced over her shoulder toward the door, then she reached for the shackles that held Wentworth's wrists, and began unlocking them. Under her breath, she whispered, "Uncle Harold—Jenkyns, you know, said the same thing. He said when the chief had used me all he wanted, he'd—he'd blind me! I don't want to be blind! Uncle Harold said I had to get you loose, and then…."

Her hands shook at her task. Over her head, Wentworth smiled at Nita. She nodded, "I might have known you were behind Jenkyns in what he did," she said.

Wentworth shook his head. He was free now and the girl moved rapidly now toward Nita. "I didn't tell him to go that far," he said. "I only said that if the enemy approached him, he was to pretend to fall in with their plans. And I wasn't sure, remembering that…."

Nita, freed of the shackles, moved to Wentworth's side and clung to his arm. "What are we going to do now?" she whispered.

"First the man in the hall," Wentworth told her. "Ram Singh!"

The Sikh stepped swiftly to his side, moving boldly despite his blindness. His face was calm, his teeth showed white against his beard. Wentworth gave a sharp command in Punjabi, the Sikh's native tongue, and Ram Singh lifted cupped hands to his forehead in assent. Then Wentworth unscrewed the light bulb from its socket.

"Sue," Wentworth called softly through the darkness. "Call the guard in the hall to come quickly. Make it sound as if you were frightened!"

The girl moved over to his side. "Oh, please," she whispered. "What are you going to do? Uncle Harold…."

"Do as I tell you!"

For a moment the girl hesitated, then she let out a frightened cry. "Come quickly!" she shouted. "Oh, help, they are…."

The outer wooden door was wrenched open and the dazzling eye of a flashlight stared in upon them. Wentworth was blinded, as were they all—except Ram Singh. Through the beam of light glittering steel flickered. The challenging cry of the guard changed into a gasp, a gurgle. The light thudded to the floor, and its ray fell upon the man, showed him clinging to the bars of the gate. The hilt of Ram Singh's knife jutted from the man's right jaw, and its blade had gone hilt-deep upward and into the brain. For thirty seconds, the guard clung to the bars, eyes staring wildly into the darkness from which had come his death, then he slid to his knees, sagged to his side.

It was the work of moments to get the keys from his body and escape the cell to free the other prisoners in the second cell. In the dimly lighted hall, they huddled together while Wentworth gave instructions.

"Moran, you take your sister and go on to Newark, get rooms

in some lodging house under assumed names," Wentworth was speaking with soft authority, "and stay there until an advertisement addressed to Harold appears in the New York Times personals. It will say, 'Out of the darkness comes light. All is forgiven. Come home.' When that appears come to my home. Understand? Obey implicitly. Not only your life, but your sister's and all of ours depend on your obeying! No matter what happens, nor what you see in the papers...."

MORAN SMILED tightly. "You can count on me," he said, "but... but Linda, sir, and Jimmy!"

Wentworth threw an arm about the shoulders of Jimmy Carroll and nodded to Linda who stood close beside Nita. "They'll be taken care of," he promised. "Sue, take Hal out of this place. Jackson, follow with Linda and the boy...."

"Aw, gee, no, Mr. Wentworth," Jimmy protested. "You're going to take a crack at the Blind Man. I know you are. And I want to help you."

Wentworth tightened his arm about the boy's shoulders. "You can help me best by getting clear," he told him warmly. "I'd be worrying for fear you'd be hurt. Go, now...."

There was rebellion in Jackson's eyes, too, but when finally the boy yielded, Jackson merely saluted and stalked off with his charges. Wentworth smiled a little, watching them go. Jackson thought he was being punished for his capture... They were all so fine and loyal—even Jenkyns, who had pretended treachery to save them. Probably he had seen that there was no escape....

Wentworth shrugged aside his thoughts. This was no time for sentiment. He turned briskly to Nita, and blind Ram Singh.

"We are going to find and destroy the Blind Man," he told them softly. "Ram Singh, you will stand at my back with your knives. Nita, you must locate and lead Jenkyns to us."

Nita came close to his side, placed her hand on his arm. Once more her lover had snatched victory from defeat. There was one more swift battle ahead, and at its end they would have removed another menace from the world—if they escaped the enemy's guns. If they escaped… Wordlessly, she flung her arms about Wentworth's neck. A moment, and then they were slipping on through the hallways, Ram Singh armed with the knives which his captors had mockingly left him, Wentworth with the guard's revolver.

They met no enemy as they made their way up the open cellar stairs and the hallway into which the door opened was empty likewise for the moment. The three slipped along it soundlessly, heard footsteps, and took refuge in an alcove. But the man entered a doorway instead of passing, and for the moment, the hum of voices rose. It died with the closing of the door.

"Remain here," Wentworth ordered softly. He stole along the hall alone until he reached the door, stood there tensely listening. For a moment only the vague muddle of men's voices reached his ear. Abruptly, even that was silenced, and there was the thud and scrape of men rising from chairs. That ceased, too, and amid a tense waiting, Wentworth heard a sound that made the cold of dread creep up his spine, that stirred the heat of anger within his veins. It was the slow, emphatic tap of the Blind Man's cane, the slow shuffle of his feet!

Hearing them, Wentworth knew quite abruptly what he

would do. When those feet came to a halt… His hand went to the revolver he had tucked into his belt. He drew it clear and stood listening. His hand closed on the doorknob. The footsteps stopped! Slowly, slowly, Wentworth turned the knob. He was about to do a thing he had never done before. He was now about to execute a man in cold blood….

But the man deserved it. God knew he did! The hundreds that had been robbed of sight! The door opened a slit and the voice of the Blind Man came to his ears!

"OUR NEXT venture," he was saying, "is two-fold. We will strike simultaneously in the section around Wilkes-Barre and Millburg. In Wilkes-Barre the Darkener will be introduced into the ventilating systems of the mines I shall designate. Around Millburg, we will use planes, and take advantage of the dust storms that are sweeping the district. It is our purpose to blind every soul in Millburg!"

Wentworth stood cold, unmoving, while the man spoke. A man could plan such things as these and yet the Spider hesitated to administer justice? He shook his head. If the Blind Man's new plans went through, the entire town of Millburg—there were twenty thousand people in that manufacturing town—would be blinded. And that would not be the end. The dust storms would sweep on eastward, bearing the Darkener with them. The dust had been known to carry for more than two hundred miles across the plains from the edge of the stricken area. Those poor devils trapped in the mines….

"The work has already begun!" The Blind Man went on. "I

have paved the way for you by making it impossible for any planes to intercept you! When this is done…."

Anger became an overwhelming force in Wentworth's breast. One shot would put an end to these devilish plans. One shot… Wentworth flung wide the door, whipped up his revolver. The Blind Man stood on a small raised platform at the far end of the room, not forty feet away. An easy shot… Wentworth laughed as he leveled the revolver. What happened to him afterward did not matter but this second the Blind Man was doomed.

Wentworth tightened his finger on the trigger and a fine wet spray struck his face! Pain, like living flame, gouged at his eyeballs. A cry of agony rose in his throat, but he fought against it. He had slumped to his knees, and realized that he was shooting, shooting. The revolver bucked in his hand. All about him men screamed and shouted.

With his tortured eyes, Wentworth tried to peer into the press of men before him, to see and kill the Blind Man and he could see nothing at all. Why, Good God, it was the Darkener! The Spider was… *blind!*

CHAPTER 14
THE DARK HOURS

EVEN IN the midst of that ghastly discovery, Wentworth did not cease to fight, but he had snapped the hammer of the revolver three times on empty shells before he realized it. Still he did not cower helpless before his enemies. He charged the men he could not see, could not even hear amid the shout-

125

ing fury that was all about. His groping fingers found a throat and closed about it fiercely. He heaved backward and pivoted, swinging the body attached to that throat. He felt the jar as the pinwheeling feet of his victim struck other enemies.

Finally words began to penetrate to him. "The lights! The lights! Turn on the lights!"

And at the cry Wentworth shouted aloud fiercely. The lights were out and that put them all on equal footing, even gave him a slight advantage. The other men, his enemies, would be seeking lights but the Spider, knowing no light could help him, would devote all his energies to battle. But who had turned out the lights? Surely, none of these men. The light was their big advantage over their blinded assailant. At the thought, Wentworth knew a thrill of hope. He was not fighting alone, then. Some one friendly to him….

"Master Dick!" a voice whispered at his elbow. "Master Dick, come with me, sir."

Something very like a sob swelled in Wentworth's throat. He knew that voice. He turned blindly, his hands groping.

"Jenkyns," he whispered. *"Jenkyns!"*

The hand that closed on his trembled a little, but there was no hesitation in Jenkyns' movements. Through the press of men who still shouted and fought against each other in their confusion, he wove a way. Men collided with them and twice hands clutched at Wentworth but the revolver which he still clutched now did service as a club, and he had reason to be glad he had not dropped it when its magazine had been exhausted.

Presently, a door shutting behind them closed down the noise of the battle, and now Wentworth heard another sound—a woman sobbing.

"Nita!" he called.

The sobs stopped, but Nita did not come into his arms. Only when he called her name again did she come slowly, gropingly, to him and he cried out sharply.

"Jenkyns, are the lights on here in this room?" He faltered before he was done with the sentence and there was a coldness in his breast that swelled and swelled until it oppressed his heart.

Jenkyns' voice was just beside him. "Yes, Master Dick," he said brokenly. "The lights are on."

Wentworth fought against the sob that strangled him. The lights were on and yet Nita, darling Nita, had been forced to grope her way into his arms. That could have only one meaning—Nita, too, was blind!

His arms closed hard about her, he buried his face in her hair. Nita's eyes, her lovely eyes….

"Master Dick," said Jenkyns, "they've stopped fighting now. I think they'll begin to search for us soon. I can hide you…."

Wentworth lifted his head to listen, and knew that Jenkyns had spoken the truth. The nature of the men's shouts now had changed. Their cries were no longer merely angry, and feet slapped hurriedly along the halls. A hand tried the knob of the door behind which they crouched, but it was locked, and the footsteps raced on.

Wentworth's lips twisted bitterly. In a little less than an hour his sight would be partially restored. After that he would have three hours of hampered, slowly fading vision before the ultimate darkness descended upon him. In that time, it would be easy to race back to his Manhattan apartment and obtain the antidote which Nita was manufacturing, but what, in the meantime, would the Blind Man do? The question was needless. The monster would know that his plans had been overheard. He would prosecute a rigorous search for the Spider and his friends, and at the same time, rush the wholesale mayhem which he planned!

NITA'S SOBBING quieted. Wentworth put his hands on her shoulders and shook her a little.

"Jenkyns, hide us," he said swiftly. "Nita, when the search has eased, you must give me the antidote you have and rush back to my home for what you have there. You will have plenty of time to save your sight, and…."

"The vial is broken," Nita gasped. "I saw you blinded, and I ran to give it to you. Then they blinded me—and I fell and broke it. There is no antidote!"

Wentworth laughed a little, and the sound was strained in his own ears. "It doesn't matter," he said quietly. "Sssh, don't cry, Nita darling. It doesn't matter. You'll have plenty of time to go to the apartment and get the antidote… Jenkyns, hide us, preferably where there's a telephone. I must give the alarm…."

In the period of dark groping that followed, Wentworth knew nothing of what they did except that at frequent intervals they crouched and waited at Jenkyns' instructions. Presently, he crawled alone into a narrow compartment that barely accommodated his body.

"You're inside one of the dressers in the butler's pantry, sir," Jenkyns whispered. "I cleared them out for just this purpose!"

Wentworth bit his lips to choke back the half hysterical laughter that rose in his throat. What chance had the Spider now, hidden in a cubbyhole in the enemy's stronghold? Even if, armed and ready, he met the Blind Man face to face he stood scarcely one chance in ten of striking him down.

After a while, Jenkyns thrust a telephone into his hands, and he lifted the handset carefully. He choked back a cry as, putting the receiver to his ear, he heard the voice that whispered over the wire. It was that of the Blind Man!

It was clear that this was an extension telephone and that the Blind Man was issuing orders. They came in a swift rush of words… a change in the formula of the Darkener so that it would kill while the victims were blind, a gassing with it of every airport along the route to Millburg and beyond; orders were to go to the forces on the west coast to do the same thing to all airports within hours of Millburg. The Blind Man would personally loose the horror on Millburg….

Wentworth covered the mouthpiece of the phone with a palm lest his harsh breathing be heard by the Blind Man.

There was still some time, Wentworth thought—still a few minutes of time. It would require fifteen minutes at least to change the formula for the Darkener—from twenty minutes to a half hour to get the Darkener over the airports. If the present Darkener was used he had at most a half hour; if the new formula, fifty minutes. The Spider had fifty minutes to save half a nation from disaster! If the airports and the men on duty there were eliminated from the battle, there would be no chance of intercepting the Blind Man's planes carrying destruction to Millburg….

"…after the Darkener is released on the airports," the Blind Man's voice went calmly on, "planes and equipment are to be destroyed. This includes army and navy fields especially. That is all. Destroy this wire and all others on the estate!"

There was a click of disconnection, and Wentworth signaled frantically for the operator. There was no time to call the police—even if Stanley Kirkpatrick would have heeded the warning. He must trust to the operator to spread the alarm. If she would believe him… But she must believe!

The operator said, "Number, please?"—and in that exact instant, the wire went dead. The Blind Man had caused the line to be destroyed!

Wentworth burst open the doors of his cubbyhole prison. "Jenkyns!" he cried. "Jenkyns, you must get me off the estate at once. I must reach a telephone! In fifty minutes…."

Jenkyns whispered urgently. "Get back, Master Dick! In God's name, be quick! They're coming!"

Wentworth scrambled to his feet, jerking the reloaded revolver from his pocket. "Ram Singh!" he called. "Thy knives!"

It must be battle now. They could not delay. He heard the instant minor explosion of the doors opening and no more than ten feet away a man cried out the alarm. A gun blasted, Ram Singh cursed gutturally, and the man's shout became a dying scream.

"FLAT ON the floor, Jenkyns," Wentworth ordered swiftly.

"Nita—Ram Singh—down!" He waited an instant, then his gun spat.

It was a queer wild fight, and Wentworth's lips shrank back from set teeth, his jaw clenched achingly as he concentrated to shoot by sound. If only he had his eyes… Far off through the building a frantic cry rang out.

"The cops! The cops!" a man shouted. "Beat it—the cops!"

Feet pounded away in retreat, and Wentworth sent two final shots speeding after them. Rapidly then he gathered Nita and Ram Singh and Jenkyns to his side.

"We go out of the estate together," he ordered swiftly. "Ram Singh, you will take the *missie sahib* to my home. Guard her with thy life. Jenkyns will go with me… Nita, as soon as you have applied the antidote to your own eyes, get a plane and come after me."

Nita clung to him. "But, Dick, your eyes…."

Wentworth's arms closed about her. "I am going to Millburg by air. You should be able to reach me in time." He knew he lied and Nita knew it, too. Millburg was a full three hours fast flying to the westward. There wasn't one chance in a hundred that Nita could reach the Fifth Avenue penthouse—and then return to overtake him before his eyes were permanently blinded… Wentworth thrust Nita from him almost roughly. "We must hurry. Jenkyns, lead us."

Jenkyns' voice was queerly strained, "Yes, Master Dick," he said. "This way, please." His tones were as formal as if he ushered a guest into the penthouse. He took Wentworth's arm and they formed a hand-locked chain, Nita and Ram Singh and Wentworth.

The shouting and the excitement about police had died, and Jenkyns led a hurried way along a hallway to steps that went downward. Once they hid in a room while men hurried past.

"Just Kirkpatrick," one of them muttered to another. "Coming to warn the chief. Seems some of the cops got wise to our hideout...."

Wentworth's lips twisted. Surely, this deed of Kirkpatrick's went beyond the pale of what fear might have forced upon him. This was abject obedience to the Blind Man's interests. The twisted lips smiled coldly. There must be an accounting soon between himself and Kirkpatrick—a fierce and final accounting....

The tug of Jenkyns' hand on his arm drew him on. The hand trembled, and Wentworth spoke reassuringly to the aged butler.

"Sue and Hal are safe outside the estate by now," he said. "Hal was always unwilling, and what Sue did in releasing us wipes out her past sins."

Jenkyns whispered, "Thank you, Master Dick, I am glad."

The flight from the estate was a stumbling maze to Wentworth. He only knew that he followed the tugging on his arm, and that Ram Singh and Nita followed, led by his own hand. Sometimes, shouts rang out distantly, and once there was a burst of gunfire, but apparently not directed at them. Finally, at Jenkyns' direction, they clambered into an automobile whose engine had a coughing, uncertain exhaust. It lurched limpingly away with them.

"Where to, Master Dick?" Jenkyns asked quietly.

"Armonk airport," Wentworth said shortly. "We have about twenty-five minutes left us before the Darkener is dropped there."

The note of the engine deepened, the car leaped and jounced. Wentworth's mouth twisted with a bitter smile. They must be doing all of forty miles an hour in their dash to rescue half a nation from torture and blindness and death! He longed achingly for the powerful Hispano, or the Daimler....

Minutes dragged past. The buzzing note of the horn sounded again and again. The car swayed erratically in passing other machines, slid twice into the ditch. A deep admiration grew in Wentworth's heart. Old Jenkyns was one of those staid drivers whose topmost speed was twenty-five miles an hour on concrete, paved roads. He was driving gallantly now, without words.

"A few miles more, sir," gasped Jenkyns after what seemed an eternity of jouncing haste. "We've about ten minutes."

YES, TEN minutes if he had estimated correctly the length of time it would take the Blind Man to strike. He had tried to be accurate.... The car lurched around a short turn, and the going became smoother. Wentworth became aware of the pulsing drone of airplane motors overhead.

"What is that?" he demanded quickly. "Those airplanes, Jenkyns, are they...?"

A distant blasting, the detonation as of light bombs, reached his ears. The rattle of the car eased, the brakes squealed to a halt.

"The Darkener, Master Dick," Jenkyns said weakly. "They are dropping it on the airport. I am sorry that we were too late."

"Drive on!" Wentworth ordered harshly. "Drive on, fast! Nita, Ram Singh, cover your eyes! Jenkyns, put on goggles, if you have them, bind them tightly so that they protect your eyes."

Wentworth leaned forward tensely, his blind face peering ahead. He cursed softly under his breath. He was beginning to see a little. He could sense a lightness that was the sunlight. He spotted the dark rush of a car fleeing past them along the road.

"I have some gas masks, sir," Jenkyns interrupted. "I thought we might use them and stole them from the Blind Man."

Wentworth shouted his pleasure and they pulled the protecting devices over their heads.

The car jolted from the pavement into the parking space beside the airport. He could hear the screaming of men now. There wouldn't be a pilot who could fly him westward to intercept the Blind Man....

So near its blast almost stunned him, a bomb let go thunderously. The car staggered and creaked to a halt.

"You hurt, Jenkyns?" Wentworth demanded sharply, his voice muffled by the mask.

Jenkyns was panting. "No, sir. Something hit the engine. It stopped."

Wentworth twisted about in the car. "I've got to take Jenkyns with me, Nita," he said swiftly. "Your eyes should permit you to drive in a few more minutes. I'm beginning to see a little." He climbed to the ground, could see the pale blur of Nita's gas mask. His hands reached out and found hers. "Hurry home, dear, then follow me."

She pressed his hands wordlessly, then Wentworth caught Jenkyns' arm. "The nearest plane!" he cried.

Talking was too much of an effort, the sound deafening within the mask, and he followed where Jenkyns led. The yellowish black of the Darkener roiled about him making it hard for his hampered eyes to see at all, but he groped his way into the cockpit of the plane which Jenkyns found, fumbled with the implements.

Fortunately, as Jenkyns shouted to him, the nose was turned into the wind. The motor caught at once from the compression starter, and Wentworth could tell from its note that it was still warm. But had the plane been refueled?

No way of telling. No time to find out—there was no gauge to show. Even as he gunned the plane forward, another of the heavy bombs burst nearby, and Wentworth knew that the order to destroy hangars and planes was being obeyed.

The ship gathered way swiftly, and Wentworth's straining eyes peered out through the dark fog of the Darkener. He could see little, but he knew the airport well. It had been used in many an emergency… The tail of the ship lifted and a few moments later he slid it into the air.…

Until that moment, he had scarcely considered the planes still circling above, but he realized now that the instant he cleared the fog, they would be upon him. The Blind Man had ordered that all planes be destroyed, and the Blind Man had curious ways of punishing disobedience and failure.

Their ship had a single open cockpit in which he and Jenkyns sat side by side. Jenkyns tapped on his shoulder and tugged at the gas mask. Wentworth ripped it off and Jenkyns shouted:

"Behind you, sir, a plane!"

Wentworth tried to peer backward, but found he could see little. A blur in the sky, yes, but that was not vision. He was thrown instantly into a battle for his life for the lives of thousands of people—and his eyes were unequal to the task! All he could do was run for safety, and he had not enough altitude to risk acrobatics. Tricks in the air required vision, too, the vision to watch the all-important horizon.

Desperately he did the only thing possible. He yanked the throttle wide, and leveled off in frantic flight. He kicked the rudder at intervals. That was safe enough, but it gave him little enough protection. The ship above him was sweeping in pursuit with all the momentum of a long dive....

The deep cough of machine-guns came to his ears even through the clamor of his wide-open engine and he raced on, momentarily expecting to feel the numbing shock of lead, but gradually the machine-guns faded out of his hearing.

Wentworth stiffened in amazement. He knew from the sound of the engine that it was powerful, but what kind of power plant could have outrun a diving plane?

The earth below was a sliding blur. He got the sunlight directly in his eyes and bored westward. In a little while, his vision would reach its maximum clarity and after that, it would fade steadily until he was stone blind. Before that time, he must find and destroy the Blind Man!

HE DID not even think of the possibility of Nita overtaking him. It came to him with a sense of shock that, even if he survived the battle ahead, this was apt to be the last fight of the Spider. A blind man could not hope to cope with the kings of the Underworld.

And Nita, how would she feel toward a blind lover? God knew she would never welcome injury to him, but through this impairment of sight, she might achieve the thing they both had dreamed of through the years; their marriage.

A bitter laugh forced itself from Wentworth's heart. It choked him and he laughed again and again. He was aware that Jenkyns watched him curiously, then he looked directly at the aged butler. He could see him with fair clarity now and abruptly he realized that his entire left arm was drenched with blood. Wounded, Jenkyns had led them all to safety from the Blind Man!

"Good God, Jenkyns," he cried, "why didn't you tell me?"

Jenkyns smiled faintly. "I still had my eyes, Master Dick."

For a moment longer, he gazed into Wentworth's eyes, then he slumped down, unconscious, in his seat.

There was little Wentworth could do for him. He braced the stick between his knees and ripped aside the clothing, tied a rough bandage about the wound. He must wait for Jenkyns' recovery. Wentworth's eyes burned into the west.

There, soon, he must meet and fight the Blind Man. It must be soon, or there would not be even the slightest hope of victory. As it was, he must fight unarmed against the twin machine-guns of the enemy's ships! He set his jaw harshly.

Then, without warning, the instrument board smashed to pieces before his eyes. Reflex action of Wentworth's stick-hand

and feet threw the plane into a barrel roll. He pulled out on the bottom of the roll and streaked back the way he had come in a reversement. His head tipped back and he caught the dark, streaking passage of a plane not twenty feet above.

It had not been quick thought that had saved him after the enemy's bullets had dissolved his instrument panel. Long hours of flying in France had done that for him. He set his craft to climb steeply, watching the enemy plane zoom with the force of its dive, whirl to dive again. Flame flickered from its twin gun muzzles.

Beside Wentworth, Jenkyns groaned and lifted his white head. He smiled faintly, stared toward the attacking ship. His words did not reach Wentworth, but the movement of his lips said, "I am ready for the end. Thank God I could right the wrong, before—" He slumped down unconscious again, and Wentworth turned back to the ship that he must conquer.

He slid out from beneath the plane's dive, gaining altitude steadily and whirled, for a moment flying on almost equal terms with the other ship before it zoomed. He stared into the other cockpit and a great shout burst from him. He could not mistake the dour lines of the face; the goggles were like the dark glasses he had worn.

The man who fought to kill him was—the Blind Man! The ship he sought to stop was that which carried the Darkener westward, to blind and slay the entire countryside!

Wentworth's shout became a battle cry. He shook his fist furiously at the Blind Man, than abruptly whirled his plane head-on for a crash into the death ship!

CHAPTER 15
DISASTER!

THE BLIND Man twisted a startled face toward Wentworth as the heavy plane roared head-on toward him. He dodged frantically but it was at once apparent that the Spider's plane was faster. Through all his writhing, twisting flight, Wentworth followed, creeping nearer, nearer. Except for his revolver, he was unarmed, and that was useless in this fight.

The Blind Man knew that, but he was terrified nonetheless, for in that first moment when the planes had rushed together, he had recognized Wentworth's intention. He knew now that the Spider would, without hesitation, ram their planes together in mid-air, sending them both to death in order to accomplish his given purpose.

Such had indeed been Wentworth's intention, but when the dodging of the Blind Man avoided that first crash, Wentworth felt the perspiration rise on his forehead. Fear stabbed through him, but not for himself. If their planes had crashed, he might have had a bare chance to jump out with a parachute and escape. But the planes would fall, and the Darkener—which the enemy ship carried in huge quantity—would be spread, like a rain from hell, over the countryside!

After that one wild dash, Wentworth knew that he could not destroy the enemy plane in the air, but he did not relent in his attack. Over and around the Blind Man's ship he whirled and darted, seeming each time determined to smash the enemy to earth.

The machine-guns of the other craft hammered at him, but he gave small opportunity for attack. Then the crucial moment came.

He dived for the Blind Man and the enemy held his course and would not dodge! It was as if he had read Wentworth's mind and knew his dilemma. At the last possible moment, the Spider was forced to twitch his ship aside. Instantly, the Blind Man whirled.

Instead of attacking, he proceeded straight away westward. Wentworth wasted no time in futile whirling about him. The Blind Man had realized the situation and called his bluff. He would push steadily westward and destroy Millburg, with his nemesis helpless on his heels!

If the Blind Man delayed action long enough, Wentworth would be blind before he struck. Yet Wentworth dared not force the battle, lest his very triumph over the Blind Man should accomplish the one thing he sought to avoid—spread the Darkener broadcast over the countryside! Helplessly, Wentworth trailed the Blind Man while the earth slid steadily eastward beneath their wings, while they drew nearer and nearer to Millburg and the minutes ticked past the brief span of vision left to the Spider.

Desperately, he sought to devise a plan of action. By radio, he called again and again for the airports in their path, though he knew in advance the futility of such action. He was not even answered!

The sky about Wentworth gradually became darker, He had to strain forward to see his instrument board, and he flicked on the lights. It was only when he realized that even the lights helped but little that he understood. His vision was fading again! Within a few brief minutes he would be blind—forever!—and still the Blind Man pushed calmly on his course, intent on his fearful destruction.

Frantically, Wentworth peered ahead. If he could swerve the enemy from his sure course, there were forest spaces to northward where the Darkener's harm would be minimized, but he had no means of accomplishing that.

God give him sight, give him strength. Was it a mirage that floated ahead there on the earth? Or were they actually near the shores of Lake Michigan?

Rigidly, Wentworth held himself in check. Until the precise moment when he was to strike, he must give no warning of his intention. He had the altitude of the Blind Man by three hundred feet. Now came a swift dive.

Painfully, he held his eyes on the shimmering something which he hoped, he prayed, was Lake Michigan. What he planned to do would call for perfect maneuvering, for a foot swerve in either direction and the planes, locked, would go spinning to destruction.

He took a last glance at the water, calculated it would take fifteen minutes for them to reach a spot over its middle, then closed his eyes. He had no way of knowing whether it would help, but at least he would not overstrain them.

Minutes dragged past and Wentworth resolutely kept his eyes closed. It was difficult even to hold the ship on an even keel that

143

way, since he must depend wholly on his sense of balance, but its erratic flight might help his plans.

To the Blind Man, it would seem that Wentworth's eyes had finally failed… When Wentworth opened his eyes, his sight was a little better and he glanced down to find that he had not been mistaken. There actually was water below, a wide stretch of it!

His mouth closed grimly, and he glanced at Jenkyns. The old butler was feebly conscious. Behind them… Good God, a plane was following! If that were a henchman of the Blind Man, all was lost. He had only one chance to strike and that was at once….

WITH THE thought, Wentworth jammed the stick forward and the tail of the ship flew up. He leveled out in a tearing dive on the Blind Man. For one second, two, the ship below did not change direction, then it shied like a frightened horse. It was too late. Tensely, Wentworth set his muscles for the crucial maneuver. What he intended to do was sweep over the other ship so closely that the cross-bar of the landing gear would strike the Blind Man in the head. That was his only chance, to kill the man. If he simply wrecked the plane, the Blind Man might loose the Darkener while his ship fell.

Now there was a scant twenty-five feet between the two planes. The Blind Man had attempted an Immelmann turn with insufficient speed and his flight went awry, his controls mushy. In another moment, he would stall and spin downward. In the precise instant of the stall, the enemy plane would be nearly stationary and perfect for the Spider's purpose.

He jockeyed his plane, pulled back on the stick to swoop

just above the other ship—and before his eyes, the Blind Man's ship went into a dive. The tail flipped up fairly in the path of Wentworth's propeller. There was no help for the thing that happened then.

The propeller clawed its way into the tail assemblage of the Blind Man's plane and, out of control, it tail-spun toward the lake five thousand feet below. Wentworth did the only thing possible. He cut the engine to keep the smashed propeller from shaking the craft to pieces. Then, he too, put the nose of his ship down. He must, must prevent the Blind Man from releasing the Darkener!

Beside him, Jenkyns tugged feebly at his arm, pointing to the rear. Wentworth chanced one swift look and saw the plane that had been coming up swiftly was now shooting after him in a headlong dive. He could not accelerate his pace. Wentworth peered toward the plane below and saw a parachute blossom beside it. It was no more than a white blur in his eyes, but he recognized it. He threw back his head and laughed, checked the revolver at his belt, then prepared to leap.

He ripped loose a cushion from the seat. It would help Jenkyns to keep afloat, then he helped the older man over the side. Time was dangerously short. Already, the Blind Man's plane had splashed into the depths of Lake Michigan.

Wentworth stood in the cockpit and yanked the rip cord of his own 'chute, felt the instant violent jerk of the opening bell. His feet slammed against the tail group of his ship, then he was free, drifting toward the blue waters of the lake.

He squinted his eyes, trying to see. Vaguely, he made out the

145

two parachutes below him. He cursed raggedly. Unless his eyes were playing him tricks, one of those parachutes, that one nearest the earth, would put its passenger down on dry land—and the Blind Man would escape!

Frantically, Wentworth worked on the shrouds of his parachute, slipping air from one side, boosting himself toward the land that reached out inviting arms to him. But he knew it was futile. He would be at least five hundred yards from the shore.

Above him, he heard the roar of a plane's engine and heard the machine guns stammer violently and he drew his revolver for a last, futile attempt at defense. He was helpless, dangling in the shrouds of his 'chute....

Incredibly, the plane flashed past him, a lifted hand saluted and with the machine guns still hammering, it roared on toward the land.

So much Wentworth made out before the cold waters of the lake enveloped him. He slashed loose the shrouds of the 'chute, dived out from under its bellying folds and trod water.

"Jenkyns!" he shouted. "Jenkyns, where are you?"

His butler's hail came to him faintly and Wentworth stroked steadily toward the sound. The world was a vague white light to him, no more than that, and he knew that soon even that vision would be taken from him. Jenkyns repeated his guiding shouts and presently, Wentworth was supporting the man with the aid of the floating cushion. Together they started toward the shore.

Presently, he became aware of voices calling encouragement and he heard the splash of oars. Minutes later, he was dragged from the water.

"Who are you?" he asked wearily. His eyes told him nothing.

"Quickly, flat on your back," a voice told him urgently, and with a sob he recognized the voice of Nita van Sloan. "Quickly, Dick, the time is so short…."

Eager hands helped him and cool liquid touched the burning of his eyeballs.

"Nita," he whispered, "Nita, did you get the Blind Man?"

"You must be quiet, Dick," Nita urged. "Quiet while I wash out your eyes."

Wentworth thrust himself up. "He got away!" he shouted. "He got away, and you stopped to help me!" He buried his face in his hands. Strong hands seized him and forced him flat on his back, and more of the cooling liquid drop-drop-dropped into his eyes.

"He ran into some woods," Nita said quietly, "and there was no landing place nearer than the beach. Some men are after him."

WENTWORTH SHUT his lips tightly. He had been so near victory, and now the last hope had been snatched from him! Those men would stand no chance against a man armed with the Darkener. Even if they overtook him, they would be made instantly helpless. All he had accomplished was the aversion of one catastrophe planned by the Blind Man. If the police had acted promptly on his warning, perhaps the coal mine district had been protected also….

"You must forgive me, darling," he whispered. "But victory was so near a few moments ago, and now it is as far away as Judgment Day. I hope I shall be able to see your face again."

147

Nita laughed softly. "Your antidote is perfect, Dick. Don't worry at all." To the men, she said, "Hurry us to the shore."

A half hour later, the bandage was removed from Wentworth's eyes and he looked about him.

His lips grew hard and cold against his teeth. He could see, yes, but the middle distance was a featureless blur and beyond that he could see only massed colors. At thirty feet, he could see a man but not his face.

"Your eyes will improve," Nita assured him hurriedly. "You said we must hurry."

Wentworth nodded without words, turned toward the plane. "Jenkyns?" he inquired abruptly.

"They've taken him to a hospital near here," Nita said. "There was a fishing colony and the men helped me. It is some of them who are chasing the Blind Man. I warned them against the Darkener—"

Nita lifted the plane smoothly from the beach and Wentworth sat staring stolidly ahead. In the moment of triumph, he had lost. Now, he must build again from the very ground. The most that he had accomplished was the destruction of a plane and a supply of the Darkener. The Blind Man....

Nita twisted about in her seat and signaled to Wentworth to put on the ear-phones. He snugged them over his ears and at once the jeering voice of the Blind Man was in his brain.

"I destroyed those fools you set on my trail, Wentworth," he said harshly. "You played your game very cleverly, but you lost, as you will always lose! I shall be in New York before you, and the entire city shall feel my power!"

"What do you mean?" Wentworth cried. He threw the switch on the radio, seeking to trace the source of the call. The Blind Man laughed.

"Do you wonder what I mean?" he asked. "I will tell you this much, Wentworth: I will fill every hospital to overflowing. I will lay the people writhing in the streets. I will destroy the entire city—and every living soul in it." The laughter was obscene, gloating.

"Wait, Wentworth. Just wait!"

CHAPTER 16
COUNCIL OF DESPAIR

WENTWORTH FUMBLED swiftly with the radio, seeking to place the direction from which the message came, but before he could succeed, the signals died. He plugged the ear-phones into Nita's circuit.

"Wide open," he ordered. "We must reach New York ahead of the Blind Man. You heard his threat."

Nita's assent was strangled. "Oh, Dick, he sounded—insane, mad!"

Wentworth reflected grimly to himself that the man might be mad, but that he had more cunning than a half dozen sane persons. He might do as he threatened, and actually loose the Darkener on New York City! Might, hell! Why, there was no question about it. At the first moment of his arrival, he would race to his headquarters to prepare the holocaust.

For a while despair gripped him, but he fought against it.

149

His brain groped swiftly with the problem ahead and he began work with his radio.

At last he got through to Kirkpatrick on the police headquarters wave-length. Kirkpatrick was his only hope of stopping the Blind Man on his landing, though God knew the hope was a feeble one.

Wentworth told Kirkpatrick that, speaking in rapid French lest his message be intercepted, urged that he set men to watch all airports around New York City and attempt to capture the Blind Man when he landed.

Kirkpatrick made no reply through long seconds, then he spoke harshly. "Why do you tell me these things?" he demanded. "Don't you know—" He broke off. "I found out that I was being slowly poisoned with antimony. It was put into a medicine that the doctor prescribed so that the unpleasant taste was hidden. The servant who had helped the plot escaped and was shot by the police. I'm much more my old self, but you shouldn't have called… You shouldn't have called me."

The disconnection was abrupt. Wentworth stared ahead of him, seeing nothing. There had been an undercurrent in Kirkpatrick's voice, as if he were talking for someone else, yet trying to convey a hidden meaning. If Kirkpatrick, thanks to Wentworth's suggestion of drugs, had discovered the poison and taken remedial measures quickly enough to counteract its effects, he might be strong enough to defy the Blind Man. God knew the penalty for that defiance would be more drastic than one man should be compelled to stand… a penalty inflicted on innocents….

Wentworth busied himself with the radio again and finally raised his own home. Jacksons crisp voice came clearly.

"I know one of their hideouts, Major," he said clearly. "I followed...."

"Not now," Wentworth interrupted harshly. "We may be overhead. Is Ram Singh there?"

Ram Singh was brought to the phone and in the Sikh's native Punjabi Wentworth gave further orders.

"I'll be there in about three hours," he concluded in English. "Be sure that the message is put on all radio stations in just three hours."

"I don't understand," Nita said to him when he had finished. "I caught some of the Punjabi, I understand that you want the hideout Jackson discovered to be destroyed, but why blame Sue Morgan? Why brand her a traitor? The Blind Man will torture her to death if he hears that, as he's bound to do. Why, I think he loves Sue Morgan. If he thinks she's a traitor, he will... Oh, I see now. You *want* him to!"

"Exactly," Wentworth said softly. "I want the Blind Man to come to my apartment where he thinks Sue Morgan is hiding. When he comes to destroy her, we—will be ready!"

THE THREE hours of the flight to New York, the race through crowded rush-hour streets to his penthouse were fraught with anxiety for Wentworth.

He heard the radio news programs tell of the destruction of an apartment building in mid-town. Bombs exploded on every floor, tearing down partitions, killing a score of men. It was a hide-out of the man behind the blindness plague, the radios said, and it had been revealed to the police by Sue Morgan. The girl, the radio said, was one of the greatest heroines of all times. She had become one of the band merely to save her brother. At the first opportunity, she had betrayed the Blind Man, who had fallen in love with her and told her many of his secrets.

"A number of prisoners of the Blind Man were freed," the radio announcer ran on, "among them the nephew of the police commissioner, Stanley Kirkpatrick. It is already rumored that this discovery will cause wide political repercussions."

The taxi's radio continued to spill the news into their ears. Armed guards formed a wall with their bodies as Wentworth and Nita hurried into his apartment house. Jackson and Ram Singh met him at the door of the penthouse.

"You have done well," Wentworth assured them gravely. "Is everything ready here?"

Jackson saluted, "Yes, Major. We just gave out to the newspapers that you were responsible for getting the story from Sue Morgan and that she was hiding here."

Wentworth laughed, sharply, eagerly. "Guns, Ram Singh!" he cried.

The Sikh glided along the hall, scarcely touching the wall with his fingertips to guide himself. He came back quickly with a pair of heavy automatics which Wentworth checked with mechanical ease, then thrust them into his belt. He strode into the drawing room and saw that a device had been built around the French doors that opened on the terrace.

It consisted of pipes with frequent perforations along their sides. The ends were attached to pressure tanks. He turned and saw that the same arrangement had been made on the main door, then he nodded again in approval.

"Nita, you sit on the couch there," he directed. "You are behind the closed door there, and the door is bullet-proof, yet will let them see you. You are, for the moment, Sue Moran. Jackson, you get at the controls of the spray. Ram Singh, bring us some drinks. We are, you see, celebrating our great victory!"

It was a tense wait, the half hour that followed. Wentworth made no effort to protect himself. He sat opposite the supposed Sue Moran and talked with her, now and then rising to refill their glasses. It might have been a needless risk, but Wentworth thought he knew the temper of the Blind Man. He would not be willing to destroy the two who had ruined him so quickly!

The end of their wait came without any warning at all.

BEHIND WENTWORTH, something thudded to the floor, burst with a muffled blast and a black cloud of the Darkener fanned up and mushroomed from the ceiling. Wentworth clasped his hands to his eyes and shouted as in agony and, at the spray device, Ram Singh twisted a valve. Through the door, three men sprang shouting. In their lead was the mendicant with the dark glasses, the absurd, battered hat with its *"I am Blind"* legend—the Blind Man himself! The others wore gas masks, but it seemed likely the dark glasses protected the eyes of their leader.

"It will eat out the entire eyeball this time, Wentworth," he snarled. "I hope it eats into your brain. If it doesn't, we will find out what molten lead will do. As for you, you little—"

He turned toward Nita and shouted in discovery, in surprise

153

and consternation. For, finding that it was not Sue Moran as he thought, he suspected instantly that the entire thing was a trap.

He glanced wildly about, saw that the sprays had turned the dark cloud of the Darkener into an innocent yellow powder on the floor, saw Ram Singh crouching forward with hand on the hilt of his knife, Jackson in the opposite doorway, gun in hand.

The Blind Man shouted in terror. He turned and ran, hands thrown wildly above his head, cane cast aside in his haste. The other two men with him went for their guns, but their hands moved with a fatal slowness and the Spider's twin automatics spoke in their faces. Above the thunder of the guns, Wentworth called out clearly.

"Thine be the vengeance, Ram Singh!"

Ram Singh's shouted laughter was a war cry. His knife glittered in a swift arc, a flight that was like a beam of light. The Blind Man screamed once more, terribly. He caught the edge of the open French door between his two hands and clung there, screaming.

The spray from over the door struck fairly in his face and beneath its pelting, the glasses disappeared and the twisted lines of his make-up vanished. For just a moment, his real face stared at them before the spray finished its work and destroyed that, too, sponged the bones clean of flesh. It was the face of Walter Smythe, the financier and stock broker who had seemed to suffer most from the raids of the Blind Man, but might also by that means have looted the companies in which he was interested!

The wretched, faceless thing that had been the Blind Man

slumped to the floor and Wentworth ordered Ram Singh quietly to turn off the spray.

"We didn't have time to distill the antidote, Major," Jackson said heavily. "We had to use it in its acid form."

Wentworth turned away from the dead men on the floor, drew Nita to her feet and led her through the music room to the terrace. The late summer dusk was just drawing its veil across the heavens. Buildings were stenciled against them in black and gold.

"Thank God," Nita whispered. "Oh, thank God we both have eyes with which to see all this beauty."

Wentworth laughed, a little shakily, and drew her into his arms. "Thank God for eyes to see... *you,*" he said.